N O T E S

F R O M

U N D E R G R O U N D

N O T E S

F R O M

U N D E R G R O U N D

Eric Bogosian

HYPERION

N E W   Y O R K

Copyright © 1993 Eric Bogosian

All rights reserved. No part of this book may be used or reproduced in any manner whatsoever without written permission of the Publisher. Printed in the United States of America. For information address Hyperion, 114 Fifth Avenue, New York, New York 10011

Library of Congress Cataloging-in-Publication Data
Bogosian, Eric.
Notes from underground/Eric Bogosian
p. cm.   ISBN 1-56282-884-3
I. Title.   PS3552.O46N6   1993
813'.54—dc20   92-35191
CIP

FIRST EDITION
10 9 8 7 6 5 4 3 2 1

For George

Notes from Underground and *Scenes from the New World* are the result of various enterprises dating back to 1980 when I staged a fourteen-character play, *The New World* (with music by Glenn Branca), at Dance Theater Workshop. Along the way, some people have been key to the making of these two pieces.

Thanks to my director, Jo Bonney.

Thanks to David White, Andre Bishop and Playwrights Horizons, Roselee Goldberg, the Museum of Modern Art, Mark Russell, and Performance Space 122.

I would like to thank Arlene Donovan and Patty Detroit for their support on *Notes . . .*

And special thanks to Fyodor Dostoyevsky and Tom Miller for guidance and inspiration.

CONTENTS

NOTES

FROM

UNDERGROUND

MARCH 23

Today I ate a meal at a fancy restaurant. I like to do that sometimes. It makes me feel like I'm part of the world. Makes me realize nothing is impossible.

A man sat near me. He was wearing a ponytail. The waiter came and said: "Yes sir." The man said: "Yes. Do you have a salad? I'm not supposed to be eating." And the waiter said: "A very nice arugula." The man said: "Arugula? No, no more arugula, if I have one more piece of arugula I'm going to die. What sort of plain fish do you have?" And the waiter said: "A very nice monkfish." And the man said: "Is it an oily fish?" And the waiter said: "I can ask." And the man said: "How does it come?" And the waiter said: "With capers and sun-dried tomatoes. It is very nice." And the man looked troubled and paused and bit his lower lip and squinted his eyes a little as if he were trying to see the waiter better, then he said: "All right, I guess I'll have that."

I was very impressed by the man because he seemed to be comfortable with who he was. He belonged to something, he was part of something bigger. He knew his place.

I don't know my place. I wish I did.

MARCH 24

Sometimes I feel like I know what life is. I can feel it. I think, this is what Zen masters feel. For one moment, I feel like it all makes sense. Even the parts I don't understand. I could be walking down the street and see a piece of old chewing gum stuck to the sidewalk and think, "There's my friend, the old piece of chewing gum." I feel like I know it.

I'll see someone in his car, stopped at a stop light, and I'll think, "That person is warm and happy in his car. I'm glad he is warm and happy. He bought his car, he drives it, he is happy." Sometimes I feel so good about everything I even sing a little song to myself, something by the Beatles or Tony Bennett, or maybe just hum the theme song to the CBS Evening News with Dan Rather. I can be walking along and there it is. Just like that. Even a piece of shit on the sidewalk can make me feel good. I think: "Someone has a dog. Isn't that nice?"

It's a feeling. It doesn't last. Like the first puff of a cigarette in the morning or the first sip of a cold glass of water.

And then it's over.

MARCH 25

I listened to some people talking in the supermarket today. They were being friendly to each other. A very old man wearing a hearing aid was buying an apple. The lady behind the cash register said, "Mr. G., how are you today?" He said, "What?" and then she said, "How are you today?" He said, "I'm living." And she said, "Well, that's important." He said, "What?" And she said, "That's important." He didn't say anything after that.

It's good to be young. It's terrible to be old. When you're old, all you think about are parts of your body.

MARCH 26

I wonder what it would be like to be a criminal. Someone who does really bad things and no one knows about them. Like a spy. Or an FBI agent. People who steal cars must be like that. Working alone in the middle of the night. Like performers without an audience.

I could write something on a wall and everyone would see it but no one would know I wrote it. I could even stand there acting innocent and point at the writing and say, "Look at what someone did!"

I could stick a piece of sticky paper to someone's back in the subway and all day long they would have it sticking to them and never know. In fact I've done that. Just a small piece.

I could stand on a crowded sidewalk and not move and no one would know why.

MARCH 27

What would happen if you were so smart that you were too smart and no one could understand you? There have been people who were smarter than everyone else. Albert Einstein was like that. A genius. But what if you were even smarter than *that*? If no one could keep up with you? So you had to become stupid just so you could have someone to talk to? Would it be worth the sacrifice? Or would it be better to just stay smart and alone? But then what would be the point?

It just seems so obvious that everyone is so stupid. When I watch the evening news with Dan Rather sometimes it looks like he's smiling. Maybe because he knows it's all so stupid. He'd probably just as soon be describing the chimpanzee cage in the zoo.

Of course there really are people suffering in other countries. I guess if I lived in one of those countries he talks about and I was starving to death or being shot at, I would have a different opinion.

MARCH 27 (LATE)

I can't sleep. I tried watching television but I got frightened by all the people shooting each other.

I feel as if no one knows I'm here.

The people on TV, the actors, killing each other—everybody knows about them. I get a free ride by watching them. At least I know I'm doing something a lot of other people are doing—we're all doing it at the same time, we're all watching TV. We're all together.

But then a commercial comes on or I see a reflection of myself in the window and because I stopped for a minute I realize what I'm doing. So I turn off the TV. And now I'm just sitting in the closet writing this. I forgot how nice it is to sit in the closet with the door closed.

MARCH 28

I was thinking the other day about how much I like to eat cheddar cheese crackers. It's a passion for me. I could eat them for hours. And I'll take a handful and think, "This is the last one." But then I'll just take another handful. Then I'll think, "Now I'm going to put the box away." And then I'll eat another handful just before I close up the cardboard top. And I usually have to exert tremendous willpower just to put the box back on the shelf. I wonder if I didn't make an effort to stop eating them, if I ever would? What if I just let go and ate until I didn't want any more? Just be myself.

They must be fattening. I would get enormous like those overweight people in shopping malls who waddle around smoking cigarettes. But that wouldn't be so bad. Then I wouldn't have to think so much. I would just think, "I am fat, I wish I weren't fat anymore."

But I think like that anyway. I want to improve in many ways. I should go to therapy so I can become a better person. Life should be a continuing effort toward self-improvement. If you don't improve your life, why be alive? Then everything would be the same as it was before, so you would already know it. That would be pointless, so you have to improve.

I will make a resolution today to improve my life. I will learn people's names. I will be more disciplined. I will care about other people. I won't think negative thoughts. I won't have bad fantasies. I won't want things. I will be good.

MARCH 29

I am having difficulty concentrating. I can hardly write this down. Something is bothering me but I don't know what. I should quit smoking cigarettes but I like the way they feel.

I like the feeling of staying up very late when the world is quiet. I like to hear the tobacco sizzling inside the cigarette when I take a puff. I like to stay up late and read magazines. It's so special to look at people who don't know they are being looked at.

It wasn't always like this. Even two hundred years ago, you couldn't flip through magazines and look at fashion ads. But now, some girl comes from Ohio, arrives in New York and becomes a model. She gets photographed so we can all look at her.

I can look as much as I want. I can look at her every day, all day long if I want. If I spent that much time looking at her in real life, she'd have me arrested. Ha ha! What a joke. She doesn't even know I'm looking at her and I can look at her all I want. That's pretty funny. I can see the freckles on her skin, how her ear is shaped. I'm almost embarrassed for her. I can see the fatness of her thigh under her ski pants. Here she is, standing there modeling thermal underwear or the latest bra, and everybody can just look at her.

Some cab driver from Armenia can stare at her while he sits idling by Penn Station chewing on his greasy pastrami sandwich. He can think bad thoughts about her. Like a dog. Like Pavlov's dog; his fat little sausage grows and gets hard because some girl from Minneapolis came to New York to become an actress.

It doesn't make any difference. I don't care about cab drivers or thermal underwear. I'm just glad there are models from Minneapolis. Maybe if I look at them long enough they will send some of their inner beauty to me.

I bet they have lots of friends. In a way, I'm their friend. In a way.

MARCH 30

I love classical music. I could live in a box and if I had classical music, even on a tiny shitty radio, I would be happy because then I would know that somewhere in Germany someone was practicing his oboe. Even if I had nothing I'd be able to sleep better at night knowing that someone was really well off. Even if I could never be happy I would still be happy a little bit knowing other people are happy.

MARCH 31

Sometimes I will wake up in the morning and I will remember a dream I had where I went to a place I remember from long ago. A field with small hills and some large old trees. And after I wake up, I really miss the place. I feel sad that I haven't gone there for a long time. I think, "When I used to go there, things were easier for me." But when I try to remember exactly when I went to the place, I can't. I'm not sure I ever went there, but I miss it so much.

APRIL 1

I saw a man on the street today who had a sign that said: I'M HUNGRY, PLEASE HELP ME. So I bought him a sandwich at the store and sat with him and talked.

Although his breath was pretty bad, he was nice. But after he ate the sandwich he told me to go away. He said he was a drug addict and had to get drugs now.

I asked him if he would be there tomorrow so we could talk some more, but he said, "No, I won't be here."

I gave him a dollar to buy drugs with.

APRIL 2

I was walking along today and suddenly I realized that famous people probably have the same problems as everybody else, they probably don't have as good a time as they want everyone to believe. And a lot of poor people have a great time. But it's got to be better to have some money. Depending on what you have to do to get the money in the first place.

APRIL 4

I didn't write yesterday because I've had a really terrible sore throat. Maybe I have AIDS? It's a real possibility. I read about it all the time in the newspaper. They did a special report on the CBS Evening News with Dan Rather the other night.

Why wouldn't I get it? I should get it. If anyone's going to get it, it should be me.

I have read that it is very painful. You throw up and itch and have diarrhea endlessly but you're so weak you can't make it to the bathroom so you just shit all over yourself. You can't swallow because your throat is so sore, so you become dehydrated.

My throat isn't that sore right now, I can still drink things. But it does hurt when I sip water. It feels like I've swallowed a piece of a straight razor. It feels like the sharp piece of metal is stuck in my throat slicing into the inside of my neck and if I cough it just goes deeper and deeper and the blood starts to pour into my throat. And I start choking and coughing on the blood, but the spasms just make the piece of straight razor slice deeper into my neck.

I can see the outline of the blade pushing out under my skin. I want to pull it out. Break it through my skin and pull it out. But if I did that I would die.

So I better leave the straight razor in my throat. And try not to cough.

Dan Rather was showing us some footage of refugees in the desert who were sent canned meat from France. But the refugees sent the meat back because it was rotten and full of pus and balls of hair.

If I were hungry enough, I would eat it.

I saw another thing on TV about an old woman who went back to visit the death camp she lived in during World War II. She was Jewish, of course. She was talking about the vast crowds of people trying to get in and out of the latrine. There were only a few holes for thousands of people.

I would definitely become constipated under those conditions.

I bet the people in the concentration camps ate meat with hair in it. They probably didn't eat any meat at all. They probably just ate potatoes. Or nothing. Or grass. Or dirt. I wonder what dirt tastes like?

But I read that people live in garbage dumps in South America. I wouldn't mind that. Every day would be interesting. You'd never know what you might find. Maybe some delicacy. A broken piece of cookie at the bottom of a empty box of cookies, a dented can of ham or maybe a magazine. Probably a lot of magazines. I could just take a magazine to my little tin shack along with some day-old fried chicken and look at the pictures, smoke cigarettes, and dream. That wouldn't be so bad.

The other night on the news they were interviewing these soldiers who took a fourteen-year-old boy and stood him in front of his mother and shot him in the head. It was either in Nicaragua or Israel or something. I can't remember. I wonder what the soldiers were thinking about. What's the point of thinking about that?

In four billion years the sun will explode. But before that we'll run out of fresh water and before that we'll all die of some mutation of AIDS that's spread by coughing.

It's not my fault anyway.

I can't think about this any more today. I'm going to masturbate.

APRIL 5

I was feeling better today so I went for a walk. I saw these college students walking arm in arm. They think they are so unusual. They are so arrogant. Arm in arm watching the flowers blooming and they think they're the only people who ever lived. They know they are young and they will make love and think thoughts and be very concerned about the world. Maybe they will protest something. But in the end it doesn't make any difference. They will marry or not marry, they will have children or not have children. Certainly they will eat and they will shit. And one day, they will die.

In a hundred years or so they will be nothing. They will not be remembered by anyone, not even their grandchildren. Maybe their grandchildren. Probably they will be remembered by their grandchildren.

But they did spend some time on earth helping to destroy it with their pissing and shitting and car driving and house building.

I feel a bit better today. My sore throat is gone. But I have an itchy scab on my elbow. My landlady says I should "get it looked at." She just wants me to be in good health so I can keep paying her rent.

I would hate to lose this apartment. Not that there's anything nice about it. But it just happens to look out at other apartments, and if I turn my lights out and stand in the shadows just the right way I can watch people when they are safe at home and don't think anyone is watching them.

There's a woman who takes her clothes off and stands in front of the window with all the lights on. But she isn't very interesting except that I saw her once in the Key Food supermarket and I had to laugh to myself. I thought: "Yes, that's right, buy your toilet paper. I know what you're going to do with it!"

There's a man who sits at his kitchen table and drinks whiskey and smokes cigarettes. Usually he does this right after he's come home from being out or just before he goes out. I guess if you enjoy watching someone smoke cigarettes and drink, it's worthwhile. But I don't.

There is a man who I can't see too well. I can only see his legs and arms. A little of his mouth. He lies in bed almost every night and reads stacks of magazines. He doesn't smoke. He doesn't drink. He doesn't eat. He's very disciplined. He holds something in his hand. For a long time I couldn't figure out what he was holding. He would fondle this thing.

I went to a pawnshop and bought a little telescope. Like the pirate kind. And I got a good look at what he was touching. A small piece of baby blanket from when he was a small baby. Probably he always held it and he had an unhappy childhood. So now touching this small piece of cloth makes him happy. And it's his own special secret.

APRIL 6

I wish I could be a baby again. Then I would be innocent. Being grown-up just means being confused most of the time and unhappy all of the time. Just when things get going in a good direction, everything changes. And then I feel bad, like it's my fault everything started to go bad. And then I want to do bad things. Which doesn't help at all.

APRIL 7

I've stopped drinking coffee and I feel better already. My bowel movements have improved, probably because of the increased water in my system.

Coffee has a diuretic effect.

If I had a tumor in my rectum I wouldn't be able to think about anything else. The whole world would disappear, everything would go away except my asshole.

APRIL 8

They called from the store again. I told them I don't live here anymore, that I'm someone else. And they believed me! I can't work there anymore. Always smiling at strangers. They want you to smile all the time but they don't want you to be friendly to anyone. Even in the "Tots and Toddlers" department it's the same. I tried that for two weeks, but the situation didn't change. People like fake friendliness, but no one wants to know the *real* me. I've got savings in the bank. I don't need the aggravation.

It makes me feel a little depressed. But then I watch Dan and things are better. He understands how things are.

APRIL 9

I have been very depressed for five days. I've smoked a carton of cigarettes and masturbated about fifteen or sixteen times. Why can't life be simple like masturbation?

I love the pictures. Everybody is smiling, having a good time or at least having an orgasm.

They smile at me. They like me.

I've been thinking of maybe finding out where they publish this sex magazine I like a lot, *Club,* and then maybe going by, like I have to deliver a package and introducing myself.

In disguise of course.

And maybe one of the girls who pose in the magazine would come by. And I could just go up to her and say, "Look, I like you a lot. You have such a nice smile, you're so gentle and sweet. Would you come by my apartment for a while? And I will make you a cup of coffee. I only have instant. Or tea."

It's not that much to ask.

Maybe she'd do it.

Or maybe I would tell her I'm an artist and she would just agree to come over and sit while I drew a picture of her. And we could talk. I wouldn't touch her.

She'd never do it.

If I had a million dollars she'd do it.

If I just had a Mercedes she'd do it.

Maybe that's why I'm depressed.

I was crossing the street and I almost got hit by a man driving a Mercedes while he was talking on his car phone. He looked surprised at first and then he didn't have any expression on his face at all. He just kept talking on his phone and steered away from me. He seemed happy. Like he belonged to something.

I know what he belongs to. He belongs to the membership of people who know where they fit in, who have found a good place. Maybe they didn't find it, maybe they deserve it, or maybe they fought for it. But they have it: a Mercedes, a car phone, a credit card.

And all these people have this look of importance.

They smile a small tight smile like they have something very important on their minds and they are doing you a big favor by smiling. I bet Hitler's SS had the same look on their faces.

The man in the Mercedes knew I was beneath him. He never walks. Or he walks to get exercise, that's all.

I should join something. That's the point. Maybe a sport. Something I could do with other people. Sports are a good way to get to know people. The question is, what sport.

Too bad masturbating isn't considered a sport.

APRIL 10

After all that masturbating, I have no sex drive at all. This concerns me.

It means I'm dying. When I was younger, I could masturbate all day and I'd still want more.

But now I just stop like a dog that's been fixed. But I know what it means. It means I'm moving past my useful period as a human being. My seed-shooting period is coming to an end, and soon I will deteriorate because I am overripe and worthless.

When I am horny, I become obsessed with my prick and my balls. They become hot and I need to touch them, I need to stick them somewhere. What are they? Why do I have them?

I used to go to whores but I know that deep down they don't like me. They're very friendly at first, but now that I don't have a lot of money they're not so friendly. So that's probably why they were friendly in the first place. Having sex with a whore is just a big misunderstanding. To think of it now makes my skin crawl. To be that close to a person who's really a stranger and who doesn't really even want to talk to you is a mistake. This person would not stop to give you the correct time of day, but given the circumstances will let you push a piece of your flesh up into her flesh. And then we move around and get sweaty and I can smell her. The thought makes me nauseous. Why would I want to smell someone who won't even talk to me?

The smell comes from bacteria that she's picked up over her lifetime. Other men she's had sex with have put bacteria on her. Maybe AIDS. She doesn't know. Maybe I got AIDS from one of those whores? Probably. Who knows?

That's why porn videos were such a breakthrough. For most people, but not for me. I can't concentrate with all these people talking and moaning and squirming around. It's the acting. I can tell that they're acting. Which just points out the fact they are actors. And that is pathetic to think anybody would do this for a living! What could they be thinking of when they take the job? They were probably just lonely. They wanted a friend, and a director comes along and says: "I'll be your friend if you will star in my X-rated movie." I guess that's it.

Sometimes I look down at my prick as I finish masturbating. I look at the cum coughing out of the little hole and I think, "This is it, this is everything. This is everything in the whole world."

APRIL 11

Tax time is here. I know because Dan Rather has made it into a special theme lately.

I like Dan Rather. He seems to be friendly but concerned, and warm underneath it all. He must have a dog. Probably a labrador retriever. When he gets home at night the dog rushes up to him bobbing up and down, getting ready to spring. And Dan grabs him by the fur of his collar and crouches down and says: "Hey there boy!" and the dog tries to lick him.

I had a dream that Dan and I went for a long walk in the woods and we had long deep conversation about the general state of the world. Dan nodded and commended me on my astute observations after I spoke. Then he smiled warmly at me. We were good friends.

APRIL 11 (JUST BEFORE MIDNIGHT)

I thought about my dream when I went out for a walk. I haven't been out for quite a few days. God knows what I've been doing. Eating cheddar cheese crackers. Masturbating. Smoking. The good life. I mean it. When I was young I wanted to "be something" someday, but now I know that was a stupid idea. Being something is a lot of work for nothing. You work really hard, and then when all is said and done all you really want to do is watch television and eat cheddar cheese crackers and smoke cigarettes. So why bother in the first place?

I was walking along. It was semi-dark out. Dusk, but the street-lamps weren't on yet. I like that time of day. People are rushing home from work, but I'm going slow. Very slow. No one knows who I am. They can't really see me. I look in people's cars. See things. Boxes of tissue paper or a hat or a pair of gloves. Sometimes I just hang around a car and polish it. Get a little piece of rag and polish it as if it's my car. No one ever guesses that it's not my car. They think I'm the proud car owner. Ha! That's a good joke.

It's amazing what wearing a suit can do for you. I wear a suit and a tie and I can go into any apartment building and go to any floor. And if I ring the doorbell, people look through the peephole and open the door most of the time. If they don't I tell them that I'm a neighbor and I live in a different part of the building. Then they open the door. It's a lot of fun when they realize that they don't know me and I'm in their apartment and they really have no idea who I am.

It's a good trick.

So, I was walking tonight. And I was looking in cars. And in one car I saw a mobile phone. So I found a rag and I peed on it and I wiped all the handles of the car with that rag.

APRIL 12

Sometimes I try to watch the world being made. I will stare at a door and how it connects to the door frame and I know that it doesn't make sense. It just makes sense in my head because I've been hypnotized. Really it's just shapes and colors.

Sometimes I think I'm the only one with a mind. That in fact I am the only son of the King of the whole Universe and he (the King) made this world for my amusement. So everybody is an actor who is only here because my father told them to be here and amuse me. It's like if I come around a corner and I see a lot of people standing around in the street, I know that they're just there like movie extras to make me think this is a real street. And after I go by, they'll relax.

That's why I have such a hard time finding friends, because everyone knows I'm the son of the King and they're all afraid of me.

So what this means, if it is true, is that the world isn't real. It's fake. Someday I will catch them. If this is true. But maybe it isn't. It probably isn't.

APRIL 13

If you could really get to know someone and know that they weren't lying to you, then you would know the world was real. Because you could agree on things, you could compare notes. That must be why people get married or make art. So they'll be able to really know something and not go insane.

APRIL 14

I really feel great today. I feel like I'm breaking through something. I took a bus out to the suburbs. Somewhere in New Jersey. And then I walked through these lovely neighborhoods with sidewalks and bicycles in the front yards and shiny Mercedeses. People cutting their grass. Lots of mowed grass.

I found this split-level house. White. It had a picnic table and a swing set in the backyard.

So I went into the backyard and sat at the picnic table. It was quite lovely. I had my portable radio with me and I listened to the news.

The people came home and you should have seen the look on their faces when they saw me sitting at their picnic table.

They kept looking out the window at me.

Then the man came home. The Dad.

He opened the back door and he said in this really gruff voice: "Can I help you with something?"

I said: "No, I'm fine."

He said: "Well, if you don't mind, you're in my backyard."

I said: "I don't mind."

He said: "If I can't do anything for you, you better get going."

I said: "Can I use your bathroom?"

He thought about that one for a few minutes. I could see him asking his wife.

Of course I was wearing my suit and tie. So the man had to give me the benefit of the doubt.

Then he said: "You can use the bathroom. But make it quick and then you have to get going."

I walked into his house and I looked him in the eye and I could see that he was scared.

I went into the bathroom.

He didn't say what I could do in his bathroom. So I thought, this would be a good time to take a bath.

The man came pounding on the door after fifteen minutes went by. He unlocked the door and I was in the bathtub. He saw me naked and ran out again, I guess to call the police. He said he was going to.

I sang my song in the bathtub. I got out, dried myself off. Then I took an aspirin and brushed my teeth with the man's toothbrush. The biggest one, of course. I cleaned my hair out of the drain.

The police didn't come. The police are only people. They don't have any real power to change anything. What can they do?

I splashed some of the man's cologne on me. I got dressed and left.

When I came out of the bathroom, the whole family ran into another room and I could hear the door lock. That was funny.

I found some car keys on the kitchen table and borrowed their Volvo station wagon. I drove around, then I found a shopping mall. I left the car in the parking lot with the keys in the ignition. Let some car thief get it.

I went shopping. I bought a very sharp carbon steel kitchen knife. They are sharp, those things. And expensive. Fifteen seventy-five.

I went to a movie in the mall. I think Goldie Hawn was in it. I'm not sure because I fell asleep and woke up and the movie was over and I was all covered with popcorn bits.

I called a cab and went back to the bus station.

A great day. Exciting, invigorating. It's nice to do something constructive for a change.

APRIL 17

I got up very early in the morning and I went to the Bowery. I found a spot and stood there. I kept thinking, "This is now," but then I'd think, "No, *this* is now." But I couldn't help it, time would keep going by.

Before I knew it, four hours went by that way. I thought, "It could really be yesterday now." And I'd say to myself, "No, yesterday is over, this is today!" It's impossible to stop time. Next thing you know, you're old, then you're dead.

People would walk by me and sometimes they would look at me. They were probably thinking, "Another homeless person!" It's so easy to fool people.

After that I got on the subway, and I got off at a stop on the Upper East Side. I walked all the way down to the end of the platform and then I walked down along the narrow walkway that goes through the tunnel.

I found a spot where there was an indentation in the wall and I crouched down into it. No one knew I was there. Even when trains went by.

Even so, I found a crumpled-up gum wrapper in the corner of my cozy little spot. I just sat and thought about that gum wrapper. Who left it there? When? Where was it made? Maybe in Minneapolis. Who designed it? Where did the paper come from? Where did the gum come from? Some African country? Where did the mint in the gum come from? Where is the gum now? Maybe it's stuck on a sidewalk somewhere where thousands of people see it every day.

So where is the gum? Where is the person who wrapped it up? Where is the man who sapped the gum out of a tropical tree? Where is the man who chewed the gum? I think if I could find these people, we would be good friends.

APRIL 23

Shakespeare was born today. He was incredibly smart. Most people today are not as smart as he was. In fact, I don't think anyone is. I think all the smart people got very depressed and killed themselves probably a couple of generations ago. So there are no smart people left. Or if there are, like me, they're hiding out.

I think too much, that's my problem. I can never stop thinking. I think about thinking. I think about the fact that I think about thinking. Most people don't do that. Many people don't even know that they think. They're like dogs.

Like the dogs in the schoolyard fucking that just stand there jerking back and forth with their tongues hanging out like they don't know where they are. Maybe they don't.

Most people are like that. Or if they think at all, they miss the whole point. They worry about what their hair looks like or if their breasts are too small or too big. They worry about their noses.

What about just living? I was reading this book of poems by Edna St. Vincent Millay, and she said she would rather be alive no matter how sick or screwed up she was. That life under any circumstances was better than death.

APRIL 24

Today is Shirley MacLaine's birthday.

I have decided to turn over a new leaf. I bought a book on co-dependency titled: *Learning to Love Yourself and the Child Within and Living with the Love You Learn.* I've only read the first chapter but I know that it's time for a change. There are many parts of my personality that are not good. And I should try to be good. It's important. If I were good, I would be happy.

I have to remove my undesirable traits.

I'm going to stop smoking, stop masturbating, and stop eating. I've already stopped drinking coffee, so I don't have to do that. It's important that I do this to reach a more spiritual plane in my life.

I have an image in my mind of the person I want to become. I want to become a person who doesn't have any problems. I want to wake up every morning clean and fresh and smiling and walk out into the world and do what I have to do. Be a productive part of society.

I'll get a new job and I'll work with other people. We'll have coffee breaks together and enjoy each other's company. I'll buy a newspaper on the train home and read it. I'll cook a dinner, watch the news, read a novel and go to bed.

No more cheddar cheese crackers. No more dirty magazines. No more looking out the window at other people's apartments. No more cigarettes. No more listening outside other people's doors. No more searching through people's trash. No more looking into parked cars.

It's important that I do this. I have to become normal. I am only on this planet for one life and I want to become normal. I am not normal because as I now see from the book, I am co-dependent.

The book has the answer. If I explore my feelings and stop smoking cigarettes and overeating, I will get better.

Life is beautiful.

APRIL 26

I enjoyed that book so much that even though I haven't finished reading it yet (actually I'm still around the first chapter) I went back to the bookstore today and bought more books.

I bought a book of Freud's essays that looked interesting and a book by the philosopher Immanuel Kant and a book by a man named Stephen Hawking called *A Brief History of Time*. What's interesting about him is that he's in a wheelchair and still is a great thinker. I actually have quite a few books already, when I think about it. I really enjoy buying them. And I like to look at them on the bookshelf. It would be nice to have the time to read them.

APRIL 28

I am so depressed I can hardly lift the pen to write this. I'm not going
to write this.

MAY 1

May Day. Time for a revolution. I've been in the hospital for the past two days.

I was sharpening the kitchen knife I bought at the mall. Sharpening it and sharpening it. Seeing how sharp I could get it. I kept testing the sharpness. Running my finger across the blade.

I was feeling tense. Maybe it was the lack of cigarettes. They say when you quit smoking, you get tense.

I ran my finger across the blade and I cut my finger. Blood came out and smeared down along the blade. Dripping down. It didn't hurt. It just looked like it hurt. And I was fascinated. The whole experience was so . . . exhilarating. I don't know how to describe it. So I ran the blade along my palm and I cut my palm open. And blood came out of there too. And just for the sake of symmetry I ran the blade along the other palm. Which of course got the handle of the knife all sticky with the blood from the other cut palm.

Now I had two bleeding hands and I guess I got carried away so I turned my hand over and I ran the blade across the back of my hand. That blade was sharp! I cut the veins in the back of my hand wide open—they just popped open when I sliced them. Then there was a lot of vein blood. The dark kind. I got it all over everything. My clothes.

I was thinking about the Chinese death torture called the "death of a thousand cuts" where they hang you up and cut all these tiny incisions all over your body and you bleed slowly to death. It's supposed to be very painful.

But I didn't feel any pain. I felt liberated. I felt cool and serene, my hands bleeding, the sharp knife, my breath in my nostrils going faster and slower.

I was excited and calm at the same time. I could hear some music, little music far away in the back of my head.

I sliced the tops of my feet.

I was standing in a pool of my own blood and there was an excitement to this. Standing in a pool of blood. It's invigorating.

And then for some reason, I thought it would be very funny if I just poured gasoline on the floor and lit a match. Blood and fire.

But I didn't have any gasoline. So I started to crumple up some newspapers to light them and the next thing I knew I was in the hospital.

I woke up between these crisp white sheets. A TV set on a little cantilever hung over my head. Oprah Winfrey was on. I could hear people clacking and clicking down the corridor outside.

I had a bandage on each hand and on my feet. The knife was gone.

I felt good. I feel good. I'm home now. I'm writing this. I have to go back next week to talk to a counselor.

But you know, it's not good to dwell on these things. People who dwell on things are old people. One should just live. Not think.

I'm still not smoking. Still not masturbating. Still not eating. Tomorrow I'm going to sit in my room and not talk.

MAY 5

I have been sitting in my room for the past four days. I haven't spoken. I haven't eaten. I haven't smoked any cigarettes. I haven't masturbated.

I did drink some water. But I think that's allowed. I'm a new person. I have turned over a new leaf. I will eat now, but only good things. I will only eat Weight Watchers TV dinners. They are good for you. I will watch the news, watch Dan Rather. I will watch Dan Rather.

MAY 7

I am well. I enjoy being the new person. I have been watching Dan Rather. He's a good man. I love him. I love his goodness. I know he has his weaknesses, but overall he's good. He's concerned about other people. I know in his heart he's like me. Or I should say, he's like the new me, the good me. Like Dan, I care about other people. Sometimes I'm afraid I don't care enough. In fact, there are times when I really feel that if I was good enough, if I did enough, there wouldn't be so many bad things in the world. I have a feeling deep inside that what's wrong with the world is really a character flaw in me. It's me, deep down, it's me. It's my fault.

It *is* my fault.

I should do something about this.

The counselor from the outpatient clinic called yesterday. I told him I don't live here anymore but he didn't sound convinced. So I told him that I was a new person living in the apartment of the old person and that the old person had left to find work in Orlando, Florida. I promised I would call him with a new phone number as soon as the old person got one in Orlando. I almost got confused talking to the counselor like this, but I stuck to my guns and he had to go along with it.

It's all none of his business. He acts as if it is. I think he's just curious because he doesn't have much going on in his life. When I went to his office he asked me why I bought a kitchen knife, and I told him I bought it because I needed one, why else? And then he asked me if the knife reminded me of my penis. Then he asked me if my father ever had sexual relations with me.

And I thought: "I'm not the one who needs the counselor."

And now he's wondering why I moved to Orlando. That should keep him busy.

MAY 9

I still can't think of what to do.

My head is empty. It is an empty shell. Not happy, not sad.

I tried reading the book by Stephen Hawking but it made no sense. Who reads these books? If I could understand this book I would be able to solve a lot of problems.

MAY 10

I looked in the mirror today for three hours straight. I ate some peas.
I watched Dan Rather. I drank some water. I didn't talk.

MAY 11

I've decided to talk again, so I tried to call Dan Rather today at CBS News. I just wanted to say hello and the people at CBS were incredibly rude. It's very interesting that when someone who is actually a supporter, part of the same team, so to speak, simply wants to connect, to say, "You're doing a good job, Dan, keep it up," that this is almost impossible. I could hang around the studios but then what would I be, a Dan Rather groupie? I just wanted to talk to him, a simple request. Thirty seconds of his time. But no, that's not possible. He's very busy.

It's okay. I understand. I'm busy too. I'm getting busier every day. I have a lot of projects going right now. I've lost a lot of weight and it feels good to be in shape. I've lost twenty-five pounds in the last three weeks. Not bad. I exercise. That's important. Chin-ups, sit-ups, deep-knee bends. Mostly sit-ups. And I push myself. It's not enough to just exercise so that you're tired, it's important to feel the pain and push through the pain. That's when you have progress. No pain, no gain. It's important to have pain in your life. Without pain, you're lazy. It's important to push yourself all the way, try to find your limits.

I can tell when I walk down the street after I've exercised that people are looking at me differently. I can tell that they feel the power coming off of me. They become deferential. They step out of the way. I get taller. Sometimes I can feel that I'm taller than all of them. They just cluster around me like little dwarfs and I stride through them, tall and strong. "LOOK OUT LITTLE DWARFS, HERE I COME." Ha ha! Little dwarfs. That's pretty funny.

MAY 14

The wounds on my hands and feet are healing. I pick the scabs off so that there will be scars. The scars will become power centers. Two hands, two feet, one prick, and my eyes. I can beam people with these power centers. They know I can. That's why people are always looking at me. If I'm on the subway and I look up, someone's always looking at me. They know who I am.

MAY 15

This man was yelling at his poodle. He was going on and on, something like "Sit down, sit down! You silly little bitch!" He was really angry and I thought: "Why do I live in this city with all this anger?" Well, I took care of him. I put a curse on him. He will die soon.

MAY 16

I'm what you call an easygoing guy. A nice guy. As far as women are concerned, I'm a good catch.

Women are a mystery to me, though. I never know what they want. I used to date this one girl. She was the sister of this guy at work who had terrible breath. Her breath was fine, but when he talked to me I would feel like throwing up. He kept talking about his sister, so finally, just to get him to stop talking, I went out with her on a date that he arranged. We went to see *Die Hard 2* together. Then after that I guess we both figured we were going out together, so we just kept going out on dates.

She was a substitute teacher and very conservative. We would go to the movies and I would put my arm around her and feel her breast. She usually wouldn't move. She was kind of stiff in general. She never said anything. We would go to the movies, I would touch her breast, we would get an ice cream and I would walk her home. I figured that the way to get her in bed would be to be as romantic as possible. I would hug her in front of her apartment building and I would try to kiss her. But she would turn her head, or if I did get my mouth on top of hers, she would lock her jaws together and breathe really fast.

I'd say, "If you don't want to go out anymore, I'll call someone else. There are lots of other girls." But she said it wasn't that, she was just not "ready" yet. I should give her time. That was all she said. Sometimes we'd even go up to her apartment and listen to records together or watch TV. She'd get really nervous then. As soon as we entered her apartment, she would stop talking almost completely. Wouldn't say a word, except something like: "Would you like some crackers and dip?" And I'd say sure, and then we'd watch "Saturday Night Live."

One time I started to touch her on the couch while we were watching television and she kept sort of wrestling with me, at the same time watching the TV. She never took her eyes off the TV.

I knew that she had deep sexual needs. I tried the best seduction techniques, but nothing worked. I would blow on her neck, I would rub her knee, I tried to get her drunk and even got her shirt off, but she just started crying.

She was just sitting there in the middle of the floor of her apartment, "Saturday Night Live" on the TV, with just her bra on and her skirt, shit-faced, crying. Of course, when she started crying, I lost my sex drive. I started to hug her and pat her head and I kind of got her shirt back on and said I was sorry. And then she just started to whimper and her head was on my chest, we were both sitting on the floor. And then her head drooped down and she was still crying a little bit and she started to pat the cloth of my pants and then she started playing with my zipper.

She never looked at me or said anything. She just kept playing with my zipper and then she opened my pants up and started rubbing my cock and still crying and then she got my cock out which had become stiff and I'm sort of frozen and my shoulders starting to ache from the way we're sitting on the floor and then she did it.

She started sucking on me. Her head just bobbed up and down, up and down, real nice and slow like she was loving it. I think she was still crying a little bit. And on the TV, Eddie Murphy was smiling and pretending he was Buckwheat and here's this schoolteacher doing this. With me.

After a while I started to lose my ability to concentrate on Eddie Murphy—I think a commercial was on anyway—and I kind of fell back with my legs still crossed and she's sucking me. I can't even see her. And then everything went white and the cum just kept shooting and shooting filling her mouth and she just kept sucking and sucking.

Like she loved me. And then I sort of spaced out and she stood up and went to the bathroom and did something and I pulled my pants up and she came back and sat next to me like nothing had happened. We were watching a commercial together. Meineke Mufflers.

I said, "That was good," and she just looked at me and gave me one of those little tight smiles that people who drive Mercedeses give you. Like she didn't really want to smile. I said, "I'm happy," and she said, "That's okay." And then she didn't say anything else and I got sleepy and I left.

The next night I said let's go out but she had something to do. The night after that, we went out and I tried to kiss her again and nothing. I said, "That was nice the other night," but she didn't say anything.

After a few weeks of trying to get her to blow me again, she started to say even less and less and then she wouldn't answer the phone.

That's pretty much the extent of my dating experience. All the same, I know I'm a good catch. I know that even with my one experience with love. And that's what's important.

MAY 18

I didn't write yesterday because I had a wonderful experience. I got up early, drank some carrot juice, did my exercises, got dressed in my suit and tie and went to Fifth Avenue. I walked around, did a little window shopping. I got in a long discussion with a clerk about whether a Patek Philippe or a Rolex is the best investment. Went to Tiffany's, picked out a thirty-five-thousand-dollar diamond and had them set it in a ring. I told them that I had left my wallet in my suite at the Carlyle and would call them later with the deposit. Hah. That was a funny one. They were shaking my hand all the way to the door.

I had walked out of Tiffany's and was thinking about lunch, and found myself in front of the Museum of Modern Art. A woman walked by me wearing a long black coat and black boots. And for some reason I followed her in and she checked her coat and I could see what she was wearing: some faded jeans, a sort of tight sweater, and a little scarf around her neck.

She looked over at me and I smiled. She sort of smiled back and then she went into the museum.

I figured it was worth the investment and I followed her in. I thought: "Isn't this exciting? It's like being in a movie!" Everywhere she went, I went. I would stare at a painting really intently and then glance at her out of the side of my eye.

If she saw me looking, I would look away.

Then one time while I was looking away she must have walked into another room, because I lost her. I tried not to seem too anxious about it, but it was a terrible loss.

All of a sudden there was a tap on my shoulder. I thought it was a guard telling me to stop following the woman around. But it wasn't a guard. It was her! My heart started to pound, my mouth became dry.

She said: "Where is Picasso's *Guernica?* Do you know?" And I said, "It's not here?" And she said, "No." And I said, "I think it's gone." She said, "Oh, that's right! I forgot!" And she smiled at me and looked into my eyes. And I looked into her eyes.

Then she said, "You're so knowledgeable about art. Do you come to the museum often?" And I said, "Only when I'm in New York. I'm staying at the Carlyle, so it's convenient." And she smiled some more. I said, "Do you come to the museum often?" And she said, "Once in a while, when I'm down." I asked her what she was down about, and she said, "Nothing." I looked at my watch and said it was lunchtime, would she have lunch with me, and she said she'd love to. So we went to the lunch room in the museum.

It was very pleasant. We talked about the Carlyle, about her job (she's a designer at an ad agency), about exercise, about my job at CBS News and my friendship with Dan Rather.

The whole time we were talking, I realized I could look at her all I wanted. She was pretty in an over-thirty way. Her eyes seemed a little tired, but bright still. She had a little hair on her upper lip but that was compensated by the large size of her breasts.

Her hair had some kind of bleach or lightener in it and she was wearing a pin that looked like a salamander all covered with diamonds. Her fingertips were perfectly manicured.

Along with lunch, she had a white wine and after lunch she smoked a cigarette. I could tell by the way she sucked on the cigarette that she was very horny. Why else would she be in the museum in the first place?

We laughed small laughs and when the check came I pretended to have forgotten my wallet. She seemed a little flustered, but paid the check anyway.

When we left, I asked her if she'd ever seen the Carlyle. She said no, and we took a walk up Madison Avenue to see it.

Outside the building, I insisted on paying her back for the meal. I said my wallet was right up in my room, let's go up.

When we got there, we just walked in, went to the elevator, and told the elevator man we wanted to go to the eleventh floor. He took us right up there and I found a room with a maid fixing it up.

I told the maid she didn't have to vacuum and we walked in and closed the door.

I broke the seal and opened the little refrigerator and gave her a beer. She took off her jacket and sat down on the couch.

She said, "You must do this all the time."

I said, "This is the first time."

I walked over to her and pulled her up to me. Our faces were very close and I could see the tiny hairs on her lip, her lipstick stain, the mascara on her eyelashes. She looked at me expectantly.

I looked into her eyes and told her to go into the bedroom. I said I had to call my office and I would be right in.

She went into the bedroom. I watched her as she started to undress. She seemed uncertain. I smiled at her and she kept going. I closed the door.

I called the front desk and told them to send up the repairman because my television set wasn't working. I told them I had to go out for an hour and wanted it fixed by the time I got back.

I left.

I went home and made a really hot bath. I thought about the woman and the TV repairman coming in. I got out a can of shave cream and covered my whole body with cream.

Then I jumped into the hot tub of water and fell asleep.

Life is good if you're willing to work at it.

MAY 20

The weather is beautiful outside. I spend all day in the park, following people around, looking in cars, sneaking into buildings. It's important to stay active.

What's the difference between being alive and being dead? Doing things. That's why it's important to do as many things as you can. It's like building a savings account of life: do lots of things and you have a big savings account, don't do many things and you are poor. It isn't enough just to think about doing things because then if you forget what you were thinking about, they didn't happen. Of course, you could really do things and then get amnesia and it would be the same thing.

MAY 25

I keep forgetting to write. Not that I care. What difference does it make whether I write or not? What difference does it make whether I'm alive or not? It's a bad attitude, I know. I should have a better attitude.

MAY 28

I'm getting older. I can feel it. Every day connects to the day before and I wonder, why am I alive. What's the point? Sure, I'm having fun. Sure I'm good now, I exercise, I've stopped smoking, I look forward to each day. But what difference does it make in the long run? I don't even watch Dan Rather. He knows it doesn't make any difference. Every day there's more bad news and it all adds up to nothing. There's this quiver of hope in his voice, that things are getting better and we should all have faith, but in fact we all know that it's pointless.

Maybe I should do charity work. Help other people. But people who do charity work only do it because they want to believe that there is good in the world. They want to believe it so badly, they do the good themselves, just to prove it. In the long run, it's selfish.

I don't want to be selfish. I want to love. I don't want to be an animal. I don't want to be a sickness.

Human beings are a virus. The history of the world is the history of destruction. It is not a history of progress. Only in a few countries. It is a history of more and more people destroying more and more fertile land, getting crowded together, fucking each other over, catching plagues, then starting again.

When the whole world is covered with people, crowded together so they can't even move, shitting and pissing all over one another, sticking knives in each other, killing every beautiful living thing, making ugly highways and buildings, abandoning the old ones to clear more land, poisoning everything they touch. When we are elbow to elbow in our own filth and can hardly breathe because the air stinks so bad, there will still be Dan Rather to tell us about it.

JUNE 1

Summer is coming, I can feel it. But I have stopped. I am like a watch that needs to be wound. I have lost interest in everything. I can't even masturbate. Yesterday I just sat in my room pushing pins into my fingers and it didn't bother me at all.

I reach a clarity and I see what I am. I am some bones and water and muscle and I take up space. That's it. It frees me to see this. But as soon as I see this and feel elated, the next thing I know I am terrifically depressed because I don't want to be just this. I want to connect to something.

I tried music. I listen to Mozart on my radio. But I've heard it too many times. I bought a quart of vodka and drank the whole thing, but nothing happened. I threw up. I banged my head on the floor.

I'm only on this earth for a certain amount of time. The clock is ticking. What's going to happen? I will die and I will not have made a mark, I will not have existed.

I think I will do some exercises. This is hard to think about.

JUNE 2

I exercise, I eat very little. I think. I walk.

JUNE 3

The solution lies in the future. If I can connect to the future, then everything will be all right. I have to connect to the future.

JUNE 4

I slept late today. I walked over to a school a few blocks over. Some
small children are there. I watched them play. It improved my mood.
I feel hope.

JUNE 5

Children are wonderful. They have wonderful energy. They are at peace with themselves. I like children.

I watched the children for an hour today. I think I will go back tomorrow.

JUNE 6

I exercised. I watched the children in the day-care center for about an hour again.

JUNE 7

I watched the children and a teacher came over and talked to me. She introduced me to a little boy, Tim. Very sweet kid. For no reason at all he came over and hugged me.

JUNE 8

I talked to the teacher again today. Told her about my job at CBS News, how I travel a lot and stay at the Carlyle. She was surprised to find me in this neighborhood. I told her my sister lived nearby. We talked about the kids. Tim came by and said hello.

I think the teacher—her name is Wanda—wants me to ask her on a date. (Of course I was wearing my suit and tie!)

JUNE 9

I stayed in today.

JUNE 10

I could kill myself. But that's so redundant. It's going to happen anyway.

JUNE 11

Went by and saw Wanda and the kids. Wanda definitely wants some action.

JUNE 12

Little Tim introduced me to his little sister today. Her name is Em-meta. I think that's what he said. I never heard that name before. Tim is five, his sister is three. They are both very sweet. We had a long conversation about cookies.

JUNE 13

I brought some Chips Ahoy to the schoolyard today and snuck them to Tim and Emmeta. They're going to be my friends for life. Wanda came by and told me she only watches CBS News now. I told her she has good taste and she laughed.

She's sweet.

JUNE 14

School ends in a few days. My life is starting up again.

JUNE 16

Tim and Emmeta are with me now. They're in the next room eating cookies. They're so sweet.

JUNE 17 (EARLY)

Tim and Emmeta are still sleeping from the sleeping pills I put in their juice. They look like two angels, so nice and clean after their morning bath.

Fortunately, no one knows me in this building, and I'm about twenty blocks from the school so there's not much chance they're going to find us. I'd like to see Wanda's face. She'd never suspect.

(AFTERNOON)

The kids are sleeping. I'm making dinner for them when they wake up. I called the school and asked if there was any news about the missing children. The person who answered the phone asked me who I was, so I hung up. Once you hang up, they can't find you.

(LATER)

I don't know what to do. The kids aren't waking up. I can't sleep.

JUNE 18

Good news! I had fallen asleep, waiting for the kids to wake up. Around ten o'clock Emmeta was touching my face and woke *me* up. She said she wanted her mommy. I asked her if she was thirsty and she said, "Yes," so I got her a glass of juice. Tim woke up and we all sat around talking about his mommy and where she might be. I gave them more cookies, then I told them to go to sleep and we would all try and find their mommy in the morning.

JUNE 19

What a day! It's amazing how much can happen in a day! Got up early with the kids and got them dressed and cleaned up. They're so nice. Emmeta called me Daddy but Tim told her I wasn't their daddy. I showed them a letter which I said I just got from the mailman (Tim can't read, of course) and explained that their mommy and daddy had to move to another city and we have to go find them. Tim seemed to find this an okay explanation and Emmeta does whatever Tim tells her to do.

So we took the Amtrak to Philadelphia, which has an interesting train station. Then we got a bus to Minneapolis. Right now we're in a hotel because they got too tired to go all the way to Minneapolis.

I told them we will meet their mommy and daddy in Disneyland. Which we will get to eventually. They're such nice kids. I love them so much. It's amazing how children really fix your life up, make everything all right again, when you see their faces in the morning.

The world is so full of bad feelings, so many people are unhappy. And someone might say, why would you bring children into this world?

But of course, children *are* the world, there is nothing else. Either you're a child, or you're making children, or you're caring for children. That's all there is. That's what life is. I realize that was what was missing from my life. Children.

And they don't want much. Love, kindness, and cookies. Which I have for them. And I'm happy to give them everything because they give me everything. In a child's smile is everything that's good in the universe. And I belong to them and they belong to me. I know they're real. And that's love.

As long as I don't run out of cookies and keep moving toward Disneyland, everything will be all right.

JUNE 21

Father's Day. Which seems appropriate. The children are gone. I'm not sure where they are, but I guess that's okay. What's done is done, and I loved them a lot. "What goes around comes around." I guess. No reason to dwell. They are gone.

But listen to this! After I checked out yesterday, I met this wonderful woman, Shirley, at the bus station. She was going to Vancouver, too. So we decided to travel together. I was thinking, in a hypothetical way, "What if Shirley and I got married? What if we got married and had kids?" And the more I thought about it, the more I liked the idea. Shirley is Canadian.

I have a new motto: "It's never too late to become what you might have been." I told Shirley my motto and then I asked her to marry me, right on the bus. And she said she would think about it, which to me means "Yes."

You just never know.

SCENES

FROM

THE

NEW WORLD

ACT ONE

A single streetlamp illuminates a scuffled and tattered city street. It is almost midnight. This part of town is quiet except for the occasional rat or wild dog.

The NARRATOR, *a man in suit and tie and cigarette, stands beneath the light, his features obscure. He steps out.*

NARRATOR   This is the New World. Welcome.

I live in the New World. I like it here. I go exploring every chance I get. Tonight I would like you to join me. Think of it as a scientific mission. It won't take much effort on your part—the New World is so easy to look at, it is practically voyeuristic.

Tonight, I will be your guide. I will lead you on your journey. You will examine the goods as best you can. You will savor. You will absorb. And I will make my trenchant and illuminating observations.

So . . . the New World. What is it?

Well, first of all, people live here. They have dreams and fears, hopes and hates. They love and they fight, they go to work, they drive cars, and very often they kill each other. They chew, they digest, they defecate.

Each one takes center stage in his or her personal drama, absolutely certain that he or she is living an irrevocable truth. "This is really happening!" they say to themselves all day long, as they watch the other New World dwellers, some near, some far away, going through their motions. People in the New World watch a lot of television, so they can watch as many other people as often as possible.

Two people fall in love, and then a TV show is made about two people falling in love and another two people watch the TV show, learn what to do and fall in love, and a TV show is made about those two people. And then the pattern is repeated, over and over, layers and layers of reality and fantasy are sandwiched together until it is pretty hard to tell which is which. A new reality is created by the consensus of millions.

Waves of emotion and waves of electronic emission commingle and modulate one another, like a crazy martial arts dance in which two enemies try to imitate each other, trying to get the upper hand.

This is my place, this is where I live—somewhere between real and fictitious, between death and dream.

So, come on! Enter and contribute *your* hopes and fears. Sit back, relax, and come with me . . .

(The Narrator steps into the street.)

NARRATOR   The city street is perhaps my favorite haunt. Always teeming with life, full of endless variety, the perfect place for the voyeur intent on vicarious living.

It's like being surrounded by a tremendous movie set. Every morning the set is lit, the cast is assembled, and as I make my entrance, someone shouts: "Action!" My eyes become cameras noting every gesture, every flick of emotion, every sculpted facade. The textures are so rich, so passionate, so vibrant it's hard to believe it's all real . . .

(Out of the darkness shuffles a disheveled WINO.)

WINO Excuse me, sir. Could you spare a quarter for a guy who hasn't eaten in three days?

(The Narrator barely acknowledges the Wino.)

NARRATOR Sorry . . . It's as if I live in a multi-million-dollar extravaganza, populated by hundreds, maybe thousands of extras—

WINO Please? I'm starving. A dime?

NARRATOR Sorry! . . . Uh . . . thousands of extras, sets built to exacting detail by hundreds of craftsmen laboring for years.

WINO A nickel?

NARRATOR Costumers working feverishly through the night, scene painters, make-up artists . . .
     No, that's not what I meant to say . . .

WINO A penny?

NARRATOR   I'm doing something! Can't you see that I'm working, I'm busy? And you're getting in the way! I don't have any money for you, now go get out of here!

WINO   Busy? Hey, we're all busy, pal. We're all busy. "Get out of here! Get out of here!"? *You get out of here!* You Bum! You're a BUM, you know that? *That's what you are!*

(The Wino shuffles off into a corner. He pulls out a pint of wine and drinks, swaying slightly. ANOTHER WINO *arrives on the scene and they drink together in amiable brotherhood.)*

NARRATOR   Uh . . . these . . . this massive effort is at work twenty-four hours a day, making believable a fiction crammed with dramatic emotion.

Yet, deep in my heart, I suspect these people I see around me—the winos, the hookers, the junkies, and the pimps—just hang up their costumes at the end of the day, punch the clock, and go home. There they find a warm meal and a cozy bed not unlike my own. They couldn't possibly be out there in the cold all the time. They have to get a break once in a while.

The size of this world is mind-boggling. How does it get put together every day? The buildings, the traffic, the airplanes overhead, are they real or not? Who could produce such an immense project?

I cannot accept the notion that when I crack an egg open in the morning, millions of other people are doing the same. It's impossible. Where would all the eggs come from?

Millions of eggs from millions of chickens? Millions! And then there's the bacon, think of that!

Millions of hogs, hacked into millions of bellies, chopped into billions of crispy slices of bacon to sit alongside millions of slices of toast dripping with the fat from trillions of cows. It's all a fantasy. It must be.

(As the Narrator speaks, the two Winos in the background are no longer getting along so well. They struggle over the wine bottle, then start to hit each other. They grapple behind the Narrator; too drunk to do any real damage, they are locked in a slow-motion slam-dance.)

NARRATOR   Not to mention the obviously absurd accidents that are reported daily in the newspapers and on TV. A ferry sinking in Egypt, a hurricane in Florida, a gang rape here, a scrambled four-year-old there. Thousands die in monsoon floods. I'm sorry, but there has to be some mistake. How can thousands of people die all at once? That's what my heart wants to know.

(The first Wino slips and falls, and the second, getting the upper hand, kicks the fallen Wino's head two or three times, really hard. He grabs the bottle and walks away into the gloom, leaving his pal on the ground, inert.)

NARRATOR   In my heart, my irrational heart, I have to believe that the world is more or less like the world I know, my world.

And I have to believe the people who live in this world are more or less like me. In short, it would be very, very upsetting if I really thought the world was full of people just like me, suffering that badly. My irrational, primitive heart couldn't take it. So I think they are different.

And so, believing this, I go looking for the interesting . . .

(Two black hookers—PATTI and CHERI—have entered. Cheri spits on the ground, then checks her make-up in a small mirror. Patti walks up to the Narrator and interrupts.)

PATTI   Hey, Skinny, wanna go out?

NARRATOR   Not right now, thanks.

(The Narrator returns his attention to the audience.)

NARRATOR   And so believing . . .

(Patti blows a smoke ring that envelops the Narrator's head.)

PATTI   Wanna party?

NARRATOR   No thank you. Listen, I . . .

PATTI   What you need, baby? How about a nice, silky
smooth . . .

NARRATOR   I was . . .

PATTI   . . . blow job?

NARRATOR   Maybe some other time, I'm in the middle of . . .

PATTI   You got nice eyes. What else you got? You got
something nice for me, baby? Come on, you can tell me.
Something with a little helmet?

NARRATOR   No, I'm sorry. Excuse me.

(The Narrator splits. Cheri walks up to Patti, picking her teeth.)

CHERI   Whatchoo messin' with that skinny faggot for? He just be
lookin', that's all. You touch his ass, he fall over with a heart
attack.

(The Wino, still on the ground, shudders.)

WINO   Help me.

CHERI   I could go for a slice or somethin'.

WINO   Help me!

CHERI   Pint of Remy.

WINO   *Help me!*

PATTI   Yo! Shut the fuck up!

(Patti snaps her cigarette at the Wino.)

CHERI   You got any money? Cop some Scotty? I'm freezin' here. It's either feed the Starship or feed my ass. Jus' sit down! For two minutes. Let's go to the Greek's and sit down for two minutes. Or blast a pipeful. One o' the other.

PATTI   I can't eat.

CHERI   You green, girl. You high?

PATTI   I'm all right. Four bags.

CHERI   Four bags! You know what you turning into? You turning into some kind of junkie drug addict. That hairwon kick yo' ass.

PATTI   Shit.

CHERI   Say what?

PATTI   Say, "shit!"

CHERI   Why?

PATTI   You standin' there "Scotty" this, "Scotty" that. You a crackhead ho.

CHERI   No way.

PATTI   Oh yeah.

CHERI   Uh-uh.

PATTI   Baby, I seen it a hundred times. Take it, leave it, take it, leave it, take it, take it, take it. Take it.

CHERI   You the one doin' hairwon, sister. Not me.

PATTI   I'm all right. Jus' chippin'.

CHERI   Let's go the Greek's and get some fries. Thaw my butt out. Drink some coffee.

PATTI   I ain't eatin' no fries. I eat fries, I be throwing up same time I'm getting busy. Get the puke all over some Hassid's lap. 'Sides, I gotta get some more bread together before Spoon shows up. I gotta stay out here.

CHERI   Nothin happen', baby. Shit!

(Cheri sees a car passing.)

CHERI   *Yo honey! Two on one? Hey! Hey, it's bargain time!*

(The car keeps moving. Cheri, resigned to staying out on the street for the time being, starts brushing her hair.)

PATTI   This is good, if I don't move. I'm in a good place. I shoulda just done three.

CHERI   You know I have a taste now and then. I just keep the monkey in the cage. That's all. I don't make nothin' a habit. No drug. No man. Even Freddie, I can take him and I can leave him.

PATTI   You leave Freddie, he whip yo ass.

CHERI   I'm talking psychologically I can take him or leave him. That's all. He's not a bad guy. I'm not going nowhere.

PATTI   Oh.

CHERI   So my point is, if you let me talk, is Freddie had this Persian dope last week. Brown as dirt. Strong. Real strong. I went out. I had the nicest dream. Saw all these mountains, green trees, shimmery water. One tree was taller than all the rest and a little bird sat on top, singing its brains out. 'Cause the sun was going down and everything was orangey and on fire, like. And this bird is singing and singing like it's the end of the world. Like millions of bells in millions of churches.
       And then there was this water, this, I guess it was a lake, seemed like a lake. And the water was cool and clear and I started walking into the water and the bird was singing like shit and I just kept walkin' and walkin', deeper and

deeper, and I was thinking to myself, "You must be crazy, girl! You don't know how to swim! You gonna drown yoself."

But I walked until I was under the water, it was dark and warm in the cold water. And I just stood under the water looking up at that bird singing on top of the tree, and then it started flying, like it was looking for me.

Then the next thing I knew, Freddie was slapping me, waking me up. I punched him in the mouth and he started laughing at me!

WINO   Ohhh! My head! Help me!

PATTI   Shut up!

WINO   My face!

PATTI   Shut your face! You stink like something that died. So go finish the job.

CHERI   Hey, Patti, don't be *too* nice. He'll think you be coming on to him. And girl, you can't blow something that's already blowed away.

PATTI   I've done worse.

CHERI   Come on, let's just go sit in the Greek's.

WINO   I'm not dead. You're dead. Whore!

PATTI   Say what?

WINO   Slut! Prostitute!

PATTI   Who you talkin' to, Stinky?

WINO   Strumpet!

CHERI   He wants you, Patti.

WINO   I see what you're doing. I know what you are. Whores in Babylon. Sodomites. You give 'em what they want, doncha?

PATTI   I'm a working girl, Stinky. Not a leech like you, something people gotta step over, something people gotta scrape from their shoes. Hold dere nose.

WINO   I might be garbage, but you're the garbage can. You take whatever people put in you.

(The Wino laughs. Cheri can't help but smirk.)

PATTI   And you look like cat puke and you smell. Didn't your mommy teach you how to go to the bathroom?

WINO   I'm not a godforsaken heroin addict. I'm not a crackhead. I'm not a slave to some two-toned fur-lined soft-talking animal who calls himself my boyfriend. I'm not enslaved to money. I'm a free man. HEY SLAVES! DID YOU HEAR? THEY FREED YOU, SLAVES! YOU'RE FREE. SLAVES? SLAVES?

PATTI   You the slave old man, you the goddamn slave. Slave to
that bottle. Look at you sitting in your own shit laughing
like a monkey.

CHERI   He be laughing at you, girl.

(The girls are losing interest in the Wino, still on the lookout for Johns.)

WINO   You have no idea how the world works, do you? You
think that you're some kind of special case, unique, never
before seen. You're gonna be treated the way no one's ever
been treated before. Let me tell you something, little
girls—I've been to the top and I've been to the bottom and
I've seen the gears turning and it's nothing but a *meat
grinder*. Big teeth, sharp and nasty, turning and turning.
Covered with blood, dripping down as the teeth sink into the
new victims, who get chewed and spat out.
     Those big sharp gears are always looking for new meat,
and that's what you are, that's *all* you are, new meat—

CHERI   And what are you? Old meat?

WINO   I jumped off. I pass. I'm not participating. I refuse to join
the march of the lemmings. Go vote for President. Go buy
yourself a Big Mac, watch the news, and inject opiates in
your veins. I don't need it. I'm a free man, I was born free
and I'm gonna die free. You can keep your war. I'm a
peaceful man, I stay close to the ground, so I can hear the
footsteps coming. I don't want to fight, I'm not angry at

anyone. But you, you're just cannon fodder in the war of the worlds. You've lost your souls and you're not even alive. You're standing around waiting.

(The Wino has gotten excited. He's almost standing up.)

WINO   *Next? Who's next in line?* Maybe I win, maybe I lose. Lottery or guillotine, who knows? Probably guillotine. But who knows? Maybe there's gonna be a war and I'll be vaporized. Maybe I'll become rich and famous. Believe it or not, I used to be famous. Had my own band. But I don't need any of that now, I'm done fighting. I'm livin' and sitting this one out.

(BOOTS and ANGEL lope down the sidewalk and come up to the two girls. They wear oversized everything: jackets, pants, shoes. Their laces are undone, their pants are half-open, revealing boxer shorts. Angel wears a Pirates' hat on backwards. Boots is unshaven and red-eyed, holding a wine bottle. Both are jittery with a jerky energy. Angel walks up to Cheri.)

ANGEL   Hey, Momma, lookin' good!

CHERI   Yo blood, wanna party?

BOOTS   We wanna party, babe. You wanna party?

CHERI   I love to party.

BOOTS   You wanna party, babe?

PATTI   I'm a party girl.

BOOTS   You a beautiful girl, anybody ever tell you that?

PATTI   My old man tells me that every night, right after he takes my money.

BOOTS   Your old man? Where's your old man? I don't see him here.

PATTI   He's coming. Sooner or later.

BOOTS   I don't give a shit.

ANGEL   They want to get busy, let's get busy.

CHERI   How much you boys got?

ANGEL   How much?

BOOTS   Ten inches.

CHERI   Yeah? I'm not talkin' sperm count, I'm talkin' cash flow.

BOOTS   Cash flow? I thought you liked me.

PATTI   I love you, baby, but my old man needs his cash.

BOOTS   Fuck your old man.

ANGEL   We do you like you never be done before!

PATTI   Oh yeah?

BOOTS   That right.

CHERI   We gotta work, we can't be wastin' our time on homeboys like you.

ANGEL   Never been locked up.

CHERI   Say what?

ANGEL   Ain't no punk, ain't no homeboy. Never been locked up.

BOOTS   We nice guys. We don't commit no crimes.

CHERI   Oh, I musta mistook you for somebody else.

(The Wino shouts from his spot.)

WINO   You think you know everything and you don't know your own name. You think you're kings but you have coins on your eyes. You're not even breathin'. Are you breathin'? I am. Bunch of victims. You're just a bunch of animals chewing on each other's guts. You'll all die together. With your pores wide open and your brains on fire. Dead animals, twitching.

BOOTS   Yo, watch your language, there's ladies present. *(to Patti)* Who's that? That your old man?

CHERI   That's God, hisself. He's keepin' an eye on all of us.

(Boots pulls a buck knife out and opens it.)

BOOTS   You want me to kill him? I'll cut his face off for you, right now.

PATTI   He's already dead. Don't bother.

BOOTS   No bother.

WINO   You can't kill me, you don't have the guts to kill me. You're too full of fear, too full of anger. You're shaking in your shoes. You're a blind man standing in a tunnel ten miles underground. You don't have a clue. Watch out, here comes your mother! Here comes the Man! Here comes the judge! You're shaking so hard you can't tie your shoe. How could you ever run the world? Your mind is a blank piece of toilet paper looking for something to wipe and call it inspiration.

(Angel walks back to the Wino and stands over him.)

ANGEL   You're an unhappy little guy, aren't you? Just lying there, talking all kind of shit.

WINO   Get away!

ANGEL   Look at my face.

WINO   Go on!

ANGEL   Look at me, old man.

CHERI   Don't hurt him, boy. He don't hurt nothing.

WINO   I know who I am. I own my soul!

(Angel grabs the Wino by the hair and pulls him up off the ground.)

ANGEL   You don't own shit.

WINO   "I am he that liveth, and was dead; And behold I am alive for evermore!"

PATTI   That's Bible shit he's talkin'!

CHERI   Leave him be. He's a priest.

(Angel slowly pulls out a knife.)

ANGEL   You know what your problem is, old man? You got no listening abilities. Your ears are all clogged up. Let me clean 'em for you.

(With tremendous strength, Angel pulls the Wino up by the neck and proceeds to cut off one of his ears. They struggle.

Now we notice the Narrator, standing in the shadows, holding a whiskey bottle, pouring shots and knocking them back. Finally, the Narrator steps forward and intercedes.)

NARRATOR   Hey.

(Angel instantly drops the Wino and turns on the Narrator.)

ANGEL   Say what?

NARRATOR   Nothing. I just said, "Hey."

ANGEL   That isn't what you said.

BOOTS   Nobody's talkin' to you, boy.

NARRATOR   I just thought—

BOOTS   What! What did you think?

CHERI   He's just a trick. Don't mind him.

BOOTS   Yeah?

(Cheri steps in and takes the Narrator's arm.)

CHERI   You're my friend, aren't you, baby?

NARRATOR   You want something to drink?

(Angel steps over to the Narrator, leaving the Wino completely forgotten. Patti is nodding out on heroin.)

CHERI   I don't drink whiskey.

ANGEL   I take a drink, man. *(He takes the bottle and swigs from it.)* I like your jacket. Where'd you get it?

NARRATOR   I had a tailor make it.

ANGEL   Lemme try it on.

NARRATOR   I don't think it will fit.

BOOTS   Sure it will. Let him try it on, man. Don't hurt his feelings.

NARRATOR   All right. Let me just take my wallet out.

ANGEL   You can leave it in there, no problem. *(Angel grabs the jacket.)* Nice material.

NARRATOR   Linen.

ANGEL   Boots, check this out. It goes with the pants. It's a suit.

BOOTS   Hey man, you didn't tell us this was no suit!

NARRATOR You didn't ask.

BOOTS You shouldn't lie to me, man. And don't give me none of your smart mouth, neither. If it's a suit, he needs the pants too.

NARRATOR I can't.

BOOTS "Can't"? What's "can't" mean? I don't know that word. I ask you for something, you give it to me. Extra-pronto.

CHERI Hey, honey, leave him alone now.

(Boots grabs Cheri by the hair and pulls her head down toward the ground.)

BOOTS Girl, you keep to your own shit, or you be lying on the ground next to your old man.

(Patti is walking away.)

ANGEL Hey! Hey, honey-cakes, where you goin'?

(Angel grabs her and brings her over to stand next to Cheri.)

ANGEL I thought you wanted to party?

PATTI   Not really. I'm not feelin' too good.

ANGEL   Oh, baby, don't worry about that. I be making you feel
   good. I start doggin' it you be feeling mighty good, so good
   you start barkin'.

WINO   The last shall be first!

(Angel walks over to Wino and kicks him in the teeth.)

ANGEL   Conjo!

BOOTS   Pants.

NARRATOR   This is absurd.

(The Narrator removes his pants.)

BOOTS   You the one that's "absurd," motherfucker. You be
   mindin' your own business you don't get your ass caught in
   no absurd crack.

ANGEL   Gotta have the shirt and the watch, man. The shoes. You
   can keep the socks, man. In case you got some kind of
   disease.

BOOTS   You don't got no disease, do you, bro? You do and he'll
   find you.

(Angel dresses in the Narrator's clothes, leaving his own clothes on the ground.)

ANGEL   I feel good now, I'm all dressed up! Okay, sister girl, it's party time.

CHERI   You don't got no money.

ANGEL   I give it to you free of charge.

(Angel grabs her by the back of the neck and leads her off. Boots whispers to Patti.)

BOOTS   I'm cold.

(He walks off and Patty follows silently. As Boots leaves, he kisses the Narrator. The Narrator stands in nothing but boxer shorts and socks. The Wino is motionless.
    Laughter and screams can be heard.
    The Narrator snaps out of it and tries to pull on Angel's clothing. As he struggles, a VET in a wheelchair enters. He is filthy, with greasy hair, smoking a cigarette.)

VET   Hey buddy, you got the time?

(The Narrator reflexively looks at his watch.)

NARRATOR   No.

VET   I think it's two o'clock, but I'm never sure.

NARRATOR   I have no idea what time it is. I just got mugged.

VET   Wanna drink?

(The Vet pulls out a quart of Thunderbird and swigs it.)

NARRATOR   Sure. *(Drinks)*

VET   You all right? You look a little fucked up.

NARRATOR   To be honest, I don't know.

VET   Know what you mean. I've been stuck in this chair since
1971, ever since I got a call in the middle of the night.
Usually we got the call during the day, fly in with "Puff"
(that was the name of my chopper), bang some slope ass, and
fly out. I dug it. The guns I carried could blow holes the size
of your head right through concrete, so I was fearless, man.
No fear at all. Rarely used the big guns anyway, regular
machine guns could Cuisinart that bamboo shit the gooks
lived in. Just do some rippin'—rip the roof off, rip the walls
down, rip their eyes open, rip their guts out. Sometimes lay
down some flames. It was fun—get stoned, drop acid, kill
people.
    So we get the call, night call, unusual. Somebody pissed

off a C.O. so we're supposed to go in and wipe the village. Middle of the night, real scary to all involved. But to us, just a nothing run. Fly out, kill, fly back. But we got stung in midair, we got banged in mid-bang.

I hear this boom, and I look over and there's Archie my mini-gun man, and he's not there anymore, just his head and his spine, but no chest, no stomach. He looks at me, just a head on a stick. It was nightmare time—then he flops over. Second boom, whacked right in the teeth, I'm going down. Crashed, burned, and it's been VA hospitals, rehabs, and a morphine jones ever since. *(Pause)* I think about shit a lot.

NARRATOR   Yeah, I know what you mean.

VET   No you don't. You have no idea what I mean. I was God, man. I came down out of the sky and I ended life. So what happened? God got angry with me and decided, enough of this shit, and put me down? Is that what I mean? I live in hell, 'cause God got mad at me? Am I Satan?

NARRATOR   I don't know.

VET   You don't know is right. I know. I don't want to know, but I know. I know every fucking thing that I need to know! I got taught, so I know.

NARRATOR   I've got to get going.

(The Wino is on the ground, clutching his head.)

WINO   Don't listen to him, he's full of shit. He broke his leg drinking last week and he wants you to feel sorry for him and give him money.

VET   Hey, shuttup.

(The Vet turns to the Narrator, as the Narrator finishes dressing.)

VET   Don't listen to him. He's delirious.

NARRATOR   I've got to go.

VET   Wait!

WINO   Wait!

VET   Hey!

WINO   Hey!

(Cheri stumbles in, hurt.)

CHERI   Shit!

NARRATOR   Are you okay?

CHERI   Where's Patti?

WINO   There will be great fires and gnashing of teeth!

(The Narrator reaches out and touches Cheri.)

CHERI   Don't touch me!

WINO   PUNISHMENT!

CHERI   Patti?

WINO   AN EYE FOR AN EYE!

(The Vet rolls his chair over to the Wino.)

WINO   I SAW THE SEVEN ANGELS!

(The Vet pulls out a .38 and shoots the Wino in the head.)

VET   Yo, Mama, let's go find Patti.

(Cheri pushes the Vet out. A BOY enters as they leave.)

BOY   Smokin' dope! Smokin' dope! Rock and Scotty. Right here, check it out! Set you straight!

(The Boy crosses past the Narrator and disappears into the shadows of the night, chanting into the darkness.

The Narrator watches him go, then walks up to the Wino, reaches down and picks up his limp arm. He drops it. He addresses the audience.)

NARRATOR   He's not real. You don't have to feel anything, and you don't, so there's no problem. If he were real and you saw him on the evening news, he'd be a bit more moving. Maybe. But to be honest, who cares? I don't.

(The Narrator leans over the Wino.)

NARRATOR   Terry, you can get up now, this scene is finished. Terry? Terry?

(The Narrator turns to the audience.)

NARRATOR   See, even now, we're pretending that he's real, when we all know he isn't. I'm saying "Terry," like that's the name of the actor playing the Wino. Cheap trick, I know. We all know. He's not really dead. Ha! Ha!

(The Narrator starts to walk off.)

NARRATOR   Let's leave Terry and his friends behind and go
     somewhere else. Somewhere more easily digestible. Shall we?
         Have an intermission, take a piss, whatever, buy some
     overpriced cookie out in the lobby and I'll see you in around
     fifteen minutes. Okay? Or leave the theater, go home, I don't
     care. It doesn't really make any difference.
         See you in fifteen. Maybe.

*(The Narrator walks off. The Wino is still lying inert on stage.
   The stage goes black.)*

ACT TWO

An upscale New York restaurant. White tablecloths, silver, endless waiters, vast sprays of flowers, muted lighting. Vivaldi plays softly in the background.

The place is filling up, the bustle quickens.

The Narrator enters. He's back in his suit and tie. He steps toward the audience and speaks.

NARRATOR   In contrast to the dark, wet world of the streets, *here* everything is white and dry. I like it; I like its soft texture, its hushed voice. The ghostly pallor allows me to stand out in harsh contrast as I laugh loudly and sip tiny cups of espresso. *(Laughs)*

Many people I know live in this neighborhood. They live here because people they know live here, so we're all here together. We like seeing each other here. It's cozy. It's "family."

Linen. Fresh ground pepper. Armani. Buttery leathers and limey perfumes. Harsh haircuts and displaced suntans. Mineral water, clean ashtrays, crème brûlée.

You get the idea.

(The Narrator finds an empty table and sits reading the New York Times. *A* WAITER *rushes over and serves him a steaming espresso.*

STAN *and* ELLEN, *a groomed and well-dressed business couple in their thirties, enter, led by the* MAITRE D'.)

MAITRE D'   Here we are, table for three.

(The Waiter snaps his fingers and a BUSBOY *rushes in to remove an extra, fourth table setting.)*

STAN   We'd prefer that table over there.

MAITRE D'   I'm sorry sir, that table is reserved. If you would like to wait at the bar, I can seat you at a more preferable table in about ten minutes.

STAN   I would not like to wait at the bar. We'll take this less preferable table.

MAITRE D'   Yes sir. Will there be a third?

STAN   Yeah, just leave a menu.

MAITRE D'   Very good, sir. The waiter will be right with you to take your order.

(Stan and Ellen sit. Another BUSBOY *rushes up with bread and butter. Ellen takes a piece.)*

ELLEN   New bread.

STAN   That's too bad. I liked the old bread.

ELLEN "You can't always get what you want."

STAN Not yet I can't.

(The Waiter arrives at their table. He places enormous menus before them.)

WAITER May I take a drink order?

(Stan and Ellen seem to ignore him.)

STAN The trick is to own your own restaurant. Then you can have whatever bread you want.

ELLEN And if the service is shitty, you just fire the fuckers.

(Ellen's brow suddenly furrows. She looks up at the Waiter.)

ELLEN What should I have?

WAITER We have a very nice Chardonnay this afternoon.

ELLEN I hate Chardonnay. My idea of hell is to have nothing to drink but Chardonnay.

WAITER We have a very wide selection of mineral waters.

(Ellen just stares up at him. She says nothing for a moment. It's as if she's frozen or had a stroke, then:)

ELLEN   Diet Coke.

WAITER   Very good. And you, sir?

STAN   Vodka martini. Very, very dry. Do you understand what I mean by "dry"?

WAITER   I think so, sir.

STAN   Dry.

WAITER   Yes, sir. I'll be right back for your order.

(The Waiter moves off.)

ELLEN   Since when do you drink martinis?

STAN   What would you like me to order? Beer? A Bud, maybe? White wine spritzer? I don't even like to drink, but vodka is a power drink. So I drink it. It establishes who I am.

ELLEN   With whom?

STAN   The goddamn waiter. Who else? He won't fuck with me now.

ELLEN   Makes sense.

(Ellen gets her dazed look again as she scans the room.)

ELLEN   There's no one identifiable here. Is everyone somewhere
    else?

STAN   We're early.

ELLEN   That's a mistake. We should have set lunch later, so we
    would be here when it counts.

STAN   I couldn't get a reservation for later.

ELLEN   Jesus, Stan, listen to yourself! You're ordering "power
    vodka" but you can't get a reservation for one o'clock.

STAN   And your point is?

ELLEN   Nothing.

STAN   What's the matter, you didn't come at least five times in a
    row last night?

ELLEN   Last night was delicious and powerful.

STAN   Well, remember that the next time you assault my power.

ELLEN   Yes, dear. I wonder where Robert is?

STAN   Maybe he fell in love with his cab driver.

(The Waiter arrives with the drinks. He places them before Stan and Ellen.)

WAITER   Would you like me to wait for your friend to arrive before listing the specials?

STAN   Do that.

(The Waiter leaves.)

ELLEN   By the way, thanks for lunch.

STAN   I'm happy to reward success. And even if Robert hadn't been promoted to one of the most powerful positions in the city, I wouldn't need an excuse to take my beautiful wife out for lunch. I want the world to see how lucky I am.

ELLEN   What a nice sentiment!

STAN   I'm not being nice, I'm telling the truth. You're beautiful, you're intensely intelligent, you're creative, and you fuck like a bunny.

ELLEN   Romance, how could I live without it?

STAN   You have to enjoy the perks in this life, because there isn't anything else. Underneath all the good stuff is nothing but a steady hum. "Take care of the luxuries, the necessities take care of themselves." I am celebrating today because we—you, me, Robert—are entering *phase two* on our march to wealth, fame, and glory. Nice restaurants are one of the perks, because we are the warriors being replenished on our crusade. We pause at our oasis before remounting our horses, unthanked heroes of a brave new world, leading the tattered masses to a more rewarding life.

ELLEN   Funny. Is this some new ad copy you're testing?

STAN   This is not ad copy. This is the truth.

ELLEN   Sometimes I wonder if you can tell the difference.

STAN   I can tell the difference. If I couldn't, I would be like the drug dealer doing his own stuff. I am the manipulator, and therefore I am not manipulated. Do you think they would have offered me a partnership in the second largest agency in America if I didn't know the difference?

ELLEN   No, of course not *(raising her glass)*. To the new warriors!

STAN   To the new world!

(They drink and kiss. ROBERT enters. He's around thirty and well dressed. He is trying to compose himself.)

ROBERT   Fuck the cab driver, fuck the cab, fuck the potholes, fuck the mayor, fuck panhandlers, fuck the crackheads, fuck the homeless people, fuck the stink, fuck the dirt!

ELLEN   Robert, so nice to see you!

(Robert kisses Ellen on both cheeks.)

ROBERT   Hi! Hi, Stan. Shit. Where's the waiter?

(Robert signals the Waiter.)

ROBERT   A delightful two days: fire Ross yesterday, witness the crying and wrist-slitting, etc. etc. Then today, no Phillip, everything falls on my shoulders. Total chaos. I shouldn't even be here.

STAN   Relax, you're with us.

ROBERT   I should go back.

(Robert stands. The Waiter arrives.)

WAITER   Yes, sir?

STAN   Get him a vodka martini. And get me another.

WAITER   Very good.

STAN   Robert, sit down.

ROBERT   You don't understand.

STAN   Yes, I do. Sit. Have a drink. You can go back in ten minutes. The world isn't going to stop. You're not curing cancer up there.

ROBERT   Yes I am. I'm curing cancer. It feels like I'm curing cancer. Listen to me, I'm babbling. Oh shit! I forgot to call Tina back. Great! Great!

STAN   Drink. Forget. Tina can wait.

ROBERT   Tina can't wait. That's the problem.

STAN   She can wait for you. Now.

ROBERT   I don't like that attitude.

STAN   Well, you better get used to it. You better get used to making people wait, making people kiss your ass, suck your dick, eat your shit. If you don't, you won't last long. You've been assigned to a position of power, the crown has been placed upon your head. Do not wear it lightly.

(The Waiter arrives with the drinks.)

ROBERT   Thank you.

(Robert takes a sip as he watches the Waiter's ass.)

ROBERT   Nice. *(Turning back to Stan)* Stan, you have a wonderful
imagination.

STAN   Thank you. I do.

ELLEN   We all have drinks now? May I propose a toast?

STAN   A toast!

ELLEN   To the hottest Arts & Culture editor in New York!

STAN   To the only Arts & Culture editor in New York!

ELLEN   To a long and prosperous dynasty!

ROBERT   To keeping my job past the first week!

STAN   Skol!

(They clink glasses and drink.)

ELLEN   Robert, stop it, you're the best! They need you!

STAN   Just think, he's going to have the pick of every writer in town, every illustrator, every photographer, nothing but the best. At his fingertips!

ELLEN   And you get to say what gets reviewed and who does the reviewing! You get to say what they say!

STAN   You can discover new talent!

ELLEN   You can deflate an overblown career!

STAN   You can shape the art world!

ELLEN   You can start a trend!

STAN   You will sculpt public perception!

ELLEN   You will be a mover, a shaker!

STAN   "Does the man make the times, or do the times make the man?"

ROBERT   Leave the *Times* out of this. This is only a weekly magazine, it's not the *Times*, nobody cares what we print.

STAN   No, Robert, it's not a weekly magazine, it's *the* weekly magazine. No one doesn't read it, no one dares *not* read it. You are the word.

ROBERT   I am very limited in what I can and cannot do.

STAN   *No!* For years we have sat here and complained about the
mediocrity all around us, now we—you—can do something
about it. Let's be honest here, Robert, you're not a
run-of-the-mill editor. You see and have seen more theater,
art, dance, and music than all of the critics in this city
combined. Plus you write plays yourself. You've studied
acting. You lived with a choreographer for six years. Your
mother owns a gallery. You are the *Uber*-editor!

ROBERT   Yeah, I guess I know objectively you're right. But it's
not something I sit around saying out loud. I do try to do a
good job.

ELLEN   Of course you do. Because unlike everyone else who
seems happy with what they're given, you want more. You
expect more. And you will have more. Someone like you
comes along once in a century!

STAN   Face it, Robert, you're a genius.

ELLEN   Robert, why do you think we're your friends? Because we
like your freckles? We like you because you're the best. And
that's because we're the best. And the best have to stick
together. It's like the fucking Bloomsbury group!

(The Waiter enters and stands patiently.)

ROBERT   It's not like the Bloomsbury group, Ellen. I'm an editor
and you're a casting agent. Stan's on Madison Avenue, for
crying out loud!

117

STAN   Now, now!

ELLEN   We are on the cutting edge, the front line, as it stands today! Mass media orchestration, talent integrated into software, symbol manipulation! The blood and guts of the future: information—how people think!

ROBERT   I don't think it's just the symbols being manipulated.

WAITER   May I tell you about today's specials?

STAN   Shoot.

WAITER   This afternoon the chef has prepared a trout almondine on a bed of watercress and sliced morel. If you are hungry, we are featuring a rack of lamb with wild mint, lemon and garlic, and on the lighter side, a quail egg soufflé garnished with *herbes de la maison* and Tanzanian spinach.

STAN   Gimme the lamb and another martini.

ELLEN   You're going to get drunk.

STAN   Impossible.

ROBERT   What's this mean? *(Pointing to a symbol on the menu)*

WAITER   It means the chef won a blue ribbon for creating the dish. It's very good.

ROBERT   But what is it?

WAITER   A hickory and balsam-smoked goose stuffed with Icelandic oysters and wild truffles.

ROBERT   Wild truffles? Aren't all truffles wild?

WAITER   Would you like me to ask the chef?

ROBERT   What's this?

WAITER   Wild boar steak slow-cooked in a Burgundy and Armenian currant sauce.

ROBERT   Uh-huh. This is some kind of *wild* place!

WAITER   Thank you.

ROBERT   Are you wild?

WAITER   Sometimes, sir.

ROBERT   I want something delicious. You choose.

WAITER   Me?

ROBERT   Yeah, just bring me something. *Surprise* me.

ELLEN   I'll have the soufflé.

WAITER   Another diet Coke? Some wine perhaps?

ELLEN   I'm fine.

ROBERT   A glass of Beaujolais, please.

WAITER   Yes, sir.

(The Waiter leaves.)

ROBERT   I wonder what he's thinking.

STAN   The Waiter? He's not thinking anything, he's a moron. That's why he's a waiter.

ROBERT   Yes, but does he hang to the left or the right, that's the important question.

STAN   Politically?

ROBERT   Penally. I think I'm in love.

ELLEN   He's appealing to your hunter's instincts.

ROBERT   Are you going to tell me about his hardware or his software?

ELLEN   You, the stronger animal, are stimulated when you are in the presence of the weaker, more vulnerable creature, our waiter. You want to consume him.

ROBERT   I'm not that hungry, Ellen. And I'm sure he's stronger than I am. I bet he lifts weights. I can see him standing in the morning light, stripped down to his underwear in front of a full-length mirror, doing military presses.

ELLEN   Physical strength is boring. It's high school. You are stronger where it counts, intellectually and financially. All this is obvious.

ROBERT   Why is it obvious?

STAN   He's serving *us*, remember?

ROBERT   Out of his own free choice.

ELLEN   How do you know that?

ROBERT   Why should I care. I just think he has a nice ass.

STAN   Robert, you're a hunter, admit it. Just because the object of your desire doesn't know it's prey doesn't mean it isn't. A rabbit doesn't sit around thinking of itself as some fox's dinner. You are one of the anointed, blessed by fate to roam through the garden, sampling freely.

ROBERT   Jesus Christ!

ELLEN   Think about it, Robert. (As if you never have!) The physical part, the sex stuff is really not that interesting. It's all just party games. It's the mental diversion, the hunt, that you love.

ROBERT   I like sex.

ELLEN   There are much bigger stakes than a piece of ass here or there.

ROBERT   Money?

ELLEN   Robert, you should be waiting tables! *Power!* You and I and Stan are members of the top one percent of the top one percent. We have been granted this. We have the choice, we can squander our mandate or we can fulfill it. We are alive while the rest of the world sleepwalks. We are not manual laborers, we are not starving Africans, we are not Ohio housewives—

ROBERT   Speak for yourself!

ELLEN   We are the operators! We are the mind of the world. We and our fellows think something and it happens. We are the most powerful elite in the most powerful country in the history of the world.

STAN   It's the only game left and we are the players. There's nothing else left but steering the hand basket on its way to Hell. We must realize the inevitable, that nothing can be done about the state the "others" are in, so it's up to us to be the aristocracy they look up to. At least they can have the joy of watching *our* joy.

      The protest march–granola–harmonica-in-the-hip-pocket sixties are over, "man," the I'm OK/you're OK narcissistic seventies are over, the golden eighties are going, going, gone! We're in the "systems" nineties, and we run the system!

(An older couple, FRANK WARNER and his wife JANICE, have been standing to one side, listening in to Stan's rant. He only now notices them.)

WARNER   Well said, Stan! Well said. Didn't understand a word of it! *(Chuckles)* How are you, son?

(Stan ejects from his seat.)

STAN   Mr. Warner! What are you . . . what a pleasure! Uh. Won't you join us?

WARNER   No, no, no! Sit down. We don't want to interrupt your lunch. Stan, allow me to introduce my wife Janice. Janice, this is Stan Chatham, the young man I'm always telling you about, the one who won't go home at night!

JANICE   *(with all the emotion of stewed pear)* Very nice to meet you, Stan.

STAN   Of course, yes. Let me introduce my, uh, wife, yeah wife, Ellen, and our good friend Robert Dreyfuss. Robert, this is Frank Warner, he's my senior partner. He owns the company, you could say.

WARNER   Shhh! Don't tell anybody!

ROBERT   Nice to meet you, sir.

WARNER   Ellen, a pleasure.

ELLEN   Stan is so excited about working at Warner & Simpson.
It's his dream come true.

WARNER   Well, we love having him. He's going to do very well.

(Silence.)

WARNER   We'll leave you to your dinner. Very nice meeting you,
Robert. Ellen. Stan, I'll see you on Monday.

(The Warners leave.)

STAN   Shit, I should have told him about Robert's promotion.
That would have got him.

(Stan sits.)

STAN   That's my boss.

ROBERT   He likes you. That's nice.

ELLEN   That was something, coming over to our table!

STAN   I didn't even see him come up. He scared the shit out of me. Was he listening to me?

ELLEN   I guess so.

STAN   I think I'm going to throw up.

ELLEN   Don't be ridiculous. He likes you.

STAN   But did I act all right? Do you think he thought I was pompous?

ELLEN   You mean, did you lick his asshole soundly?

STAN   Yeah?

ELLEN   Lemme see your tongue.

(Stan grabs his drink.)

STAN   He's a madman. You don't know. He only smiles when he's hurting someone.

ROBERT   His wife seemed nice.

STAN   She's a nymphomaniac. Into boys. Every three months she picks up a kid from mailroom, brings him home and blows his mind. Then she tells the Wolverine (that's what we call Warner) every wet detail, which he loves, and the poor jerk

gets canned. As if Warner gives a shit, he's got three
mistresses himself.

ROBERT   Oh, they sound like a lovely couple.

STAN   The Wolverine is into coke. Legend has it he got his first
sniff in 1970 when they were trying to get Miles Davis to
do a jingle for us.

ELLEN   Miles Davis was going to do a jingle?

STAN   1970. Need I say more? Janice is into pep pills and
Percodans. Didn't you see her zombie eyes?

ROBERT   She's a junkie?

ELLEN   Stan!

STAN   I'm not making this stuff up. Check this out: the
Wolverine's favorite thrill is getting pissed on, you know,
water sports.

ROBERT   Stop it!

STAN   He likes to play doctor with ten-year-old Puerto Rican
girls. He tells them they have to give him urine samples.

ROBERT   Stan, you're talking about your boss, your role model!

STAN   It's all true. My assistant used to work for his secretary.
She told me. After he's done playing doctor, he drinks them.
The urine samples.

ROBERT   You're badmouthing the man who writes your checks.

STAN   Everyone hates him at work. He's cheap. He has no ethics
whatsoever. He's perverted. He's ruthless. He enjoys
watching people suffer. And he sexually harasses his
secretary.

ROBERT   The worst! But isn't he a hunter too? Isn't he allowed all
this? Isn't he a god like us?

STAN   No.

ROBERT   Why not?

STAN   Because he's embedded in it, he's embedded in the material.
A god can fool around with the material world, but he's not
a slave to it. In short, he's a loser.

ROBERT   I wouldn't mind losing the way he's lost.

STAN   He's spinning his wheels.

ELLEN   How can you say that?

STAN   How much do you think old Wolverine is worth?

ELLEN   Three, four million?

STAN   If he's lucky, considering his ugly habits, including a
mother fixation on his wife. What do you think he does
with it?

ELLEN   Stocks? Real estate?

STAN   Exactly. He's got stocks and real estate. Then what?

ELLEN   I've lost you.

STAN   Spinning his wheels! Going nowhere! He's got this huge
company, but he's losing power every day. His life has no
direction. There is no dynamic to his actions. His real estate
is sitting there, he's drinking piss-water, and that's it! It's a
dead end. He's not alive, he's missing the whole thing! I'm,
that is to say, *we're* different. We're creating enduring
empires. Ten years from now, Robert will be editor-in-chief,
I'll have my own agency, and you will be producing movies.
We will be immortal, we will make a difference in the world.
People will look up at us and worship us, or even better turn
purple with envy. Who gives a fuck about throwing logs in a
fireplace in some Montana hideaway or sniffing illegal drugs
or reliving the same forbidden childhood fetish again and
again and again?

ROBERT   I do! I do! If you throw the waiter in, you've got a deal!
Money is nice, Stan, admit it!

STAN   Money! Money! The money comes with it. You think
Henry Kissinger worries about money? Spike Lee? Madonna?
Michael Jordan? Money comes with the territory! So do
houses in the country, kinky sex and hard drugs. But you
take them or leave them, do *not* be ruled by them. The losers
get ruled: Donald Trump—babes; John Belushi—drugs; J. D.
Salinger—house in the country.

(Robert laughs.)

ELLEN   He's not joking. Too much significance in your life is a liability.

STAN   It's a fluid, dynamic world. You have to stay on your toes, constantly solidifying your position. Constantly changing.

ROBERT   And what happens when you get old and can't stay on your toes?

STAN   I can't think about that.

ELLEN   You amass an army of assistants, lieutenants, whatever. You make *your* priorities *their* priorities.

ROBERT   For an example, what you do for old Wolverine?

(Pause)

ROBERT   How's your country house search going?

(The Narrator has stood up, folded his newspaper neatly, and come to stand next to Robert.)

NARRATOR   Excuse me, I couldn't help overhearing. I'm sorry to disturb your lunch, but aren't you Robert Dreyfuss?

ROBERT   Yes . . .

NARRATOR   I'm so happy to meet you. I just wanted to come over and wish you luck on your new position.

ROBERT   Thank you. That's nice of you.

NARRATOR   I love the pieces you've written. And I saw your play. It was really great. They shouldn't have closed it.

ROBERT   Thank you.

NARRATOR   You were absolutely right about Peter Sellers.

ROBERT   The director?

NARRATOR   The actor.

ROBERT   Ah!

NARRATOR   I'm a playwright myself.

ROBERT   Yes.

STAN   Oh, sweet Jesus!

NARRATOR   I've just finished a play. We're negotiating with some producers right now. I wonder—

ROBERT   —if I could read it?

NARRATOR   Yes! I'd appreciate *any* input.

ROBERT   You would?

ELLEN   Robert!

(Stan reaches over and deliberately knocks over Ellen's diet Coke.)

STAN   Oh, dear me! Look what I've done! Waiter!

ROBERT   Call my office.

NARRATOR   Do you have a special number?

ROBERT   My office. Just call the magazine.

ELLEN   You splashed me!

(Ellen stands.)

ELLEN   Where's the "Ladies"?

STAN   No problem! I'm coming with you.

(Stan stands.)

STAN   Robert, could you come along? You know more about
        stains than I do.

ROBERT   Oh, right. *(To the Narrator)* Sorry about this. Just call my office.

NARRATOR   Thank you. Thank you. Would you like my number?

(Robert is leaving.)

NARRATOR   *(To Robert's back)* I'll call you next week. Okay?

(The Narrator is left alone. The Waiter comes over.)

WAITER   Yes, sir?

NARRATOR   Go away.

WAITER   Yes, sir.

(The Waiter leaves.)

NARRATOR   And so, we end this chapter of delightful New World views. Tedious, but true in its own way. And don't worry, he'll read the play. I know his boss.

(The Narrator polishes off Stan's martini.)

NARRATOR   Have you noticed how much drinking goes on in the
New World? You have? You're very observant. Or maybe
you would like one yourself? Why don't you take a break,
get a drink, and when you get back, I'll be here.

ACT THREE

Everything is black. A spotlight cuts through the darkness and discovers the Narrator.

NARRATOR   Yes. Well. Here we are again—bladder empty, mind at ease. Maybe ready to get a move on. Ready to go home and watch the evening news. Enough of this! The point's been made. Whatever it is. So move on.

Okay, that will happen. I can guess with very accurate certainty that this will be over and something else will take its place soon enough. But we have one more visit to make.

We now visit the forge of the New World, where the dreams are hammered together. It's not fancy, it's almost humble. But from this place comes almost everything we know. Our hopes, dreams, fears, even intimate thoughts are sculpted right here. It doesn't take much more than a few telephones and some scratch pads, but just as one plus one equals two, a few phone calls, some sweat, some spleen, and a lot of gall are the catalyst for everything we know.

(Everything goes black.

Another spotlight comes up to reveal a neatly dressed young boy, TOMMY. Tommy looks apprehensive.

Suddenly pre-recorded music fills the air: a pop song with vocals and back-up. Something very popular—Michael Jackson or Madonna

*or Prince. With precision, Tommy mimes the tune, even mimes the
guitar breaks.)*

VOICE *(In the dark)* Okay, okay, we get the idea!

*(The music stops and lights come up to reveal an office. This is the office
of* SAM BARRY, *producer, who is himself seated on a couch with a pretty
woman,* SHARON, *on one side, and a worried-looking, very thin young
man,* BRIAN, *on the other. Brian has a phone at his elbow.*

Also present are Tommy's mother, ANDREA, *and his agent,*
TRUMPER, *the Narrator, who wears tinted glasses.*

The phone rings. Brian answers. Sam picks his nose.)

BRIAN Yes. He's in a meeting right now, can we call you back?

SAM Who is it?

(Everyone waits.)

BRIAN Mr. Lund.

SAM George?

BRIAN Yes.

SAM Find out where he is and I'll call him back. Tell him I'm in a
meeting.

(Brian whispers into the phone as Sam turns to Tommy.)

SAM   That was terrific . . . uh . . .

NARRATOR   Tommy.

SAM   Tommy. That was terrific, Tommy. Just spectacular! Very impressive. I enjoyed it very much, I almost want to see it again. You're going to go very far. Excuse me. Brian! You still got George?

(Brian doesn't realize he's being spoken to and is about to hang up the phone.)

SAM   DON'T HANG UP!

BRIAN   Hello? Hello? Mr. Lund? . . . He's gone.

SAM   Call him back!

(Suddenly black with fury, Sam turns to Sharon.)

SAM   Where's the coffee you were getting me two days ago? We're working here. I feel like I'm at a clambake watching the waves roll in! I should be hunting for seashells! GET THE COFFEE!

(Sharon runs off and Sam is all smiles again.)

SAM   I'm sorry, Tommy, but not everybody is as talented as you
      are. *(To the Narrator)* So what am I supposed to do with him?

NARRATOR   I thought that . . .

SAM   Oh yeah?

BRIAN   I have Mr. Lund on the line for you, Mr. Barry.

SAM   Don't think, Trumper, it stretches your skull all out of
      shape! Hold your thought, lemme get this.

(Sam picks up the phone.)

SAM   George! *(Pause)* DON'T GIVE ME THAT! I DON'T WANT TO HEAR
      IT! I'M NOT INTERESTED! NO! NO! THAT'S A LOT OF BULLSHIT!
      YOU'RE GONNA WHAT? LIKE HELL YOU ARE! IT WILL COST YOU
      MORE IN COURT THAN YOU'LL GET IN ROYALTIES IN FIFTY YEARS.
      YOU'LL WAIT? FOR WHAT? YOU'RE FUCKING WITH ME, GEORGE,
      AND I DON'T LIKE IT! DON'T BLOW ME, GEORGE! DON'T BLOW ME!
      AND DON'T GIMME A HAND JOB EITHER! IF YOU'RE GONNA FUCK
      ME, FUCK ME, BUT YOU BETTER WEAR A RUBBER, 'CAUSE YOU GET
      ME PREGNANT AND I'M LEAVING THE BABY AT YOUR DOORSTEP.
      (Pause)

It's very simple, George, you forget about this whole licensing lawsuit pipe dream of yours or you can forget about your buddy working in my factory for the next couple of years. I *will* be that angry. *Capiche?* Okay, okay. I'll talk to you tomorrow. I love you too. Say hi to Bindy. I will. Thanks. Okay. All right. 'Bye now.

(Sam hands the phone to Brian who hangs it up.)

SAM   COFFEE! Am I talking to myself here? Am I surrounded by cripples and retards?

(Sharon runs in with the coffee.)

SAM   Thank you. Good thing we weren't in the middle of an operation and I needed some *blood!*

(Sam turns to Tommy.)

SAM   Tommy, what do you think I should do with you—?

NARRATOR   We think Tommy has the potential of . . .

SAM   Potential? I'm tired of potential! I need results, I need the goods, I need the brass ring. This isn't some kind of training camp here, this isn't night school! I am not a benevolent society, Trumper, I am a man looking for a profit, looking for a means toward an end, be it financial, artistic, physical, whatever. I want it, and if I can't have it, I'm not happy. I'm not interested in "potential." We all have potential. Brian here has a lot of potential. Maybe someday, he'll learn how to answer the phone. But you can't sell potential, you can't eat potential, you can't fuck potential . . .

BRIAN   Sometimes you can.

SAM   Excuse me, Tommy, you understand what I'm saying, Tommy? *(Kindly)* You're a very nice little boy, but I've got to know what I'm supposed to do with you.

ANDREA   Tommy, answer Mr. Barry!

(Tommy looks at his shoes. The phone rings. Brian picks up.)

BRIAN   Yes? Well, Mr. Barry is in a meeting right now, can he?—

SAM   Who is it?

BRIAN   Norm Green. Wants to know about his script.

SAM   Tell him I'm in a meeting. You see, Tommy, we need people like you. Without people like you, terrifically talented people like you, this business wouldn't be worth my time. Believe me, I don't do it for the money. I say I want the

money, but I don't. Who needs money? Money just brings
more headaches. I want satisfaction. I want to know that I
helped make this world a better place. That's the kind of guy
I am. Underneath this coat of armor. But it's a battle,
Tommy. It's a goddamn battle, a battle I have to fight every
day. Relentlessly. And all I'm really trying to do is bring a
little love into this fucked-up world we live in. Excuse me.
(To Andrea) He doesn't know what "fuck," means does he?

ANDREA I should hope not!

SAM Good! *(To Tommy)* Most people you meet in this business,
Tommy, aren't like me, they're not nice people. They'll screw
your skinny ass right into the ground for two cents. They'll
ruin you. They'll wrap you in human bondage.

*(Tommy's eyes are wide open. Meanwhile, Brian has dismissed the last
call, the phone has rung again, and he's spouting the usual:)*

BRIAN Hello, the Barry Company. I'm sorry, he's in a meeting
right now, may I—

SAM Who is it?

BRIAN Paramount. Frank Macklin.

SAM Gimme the phone! Frank! How are you? Yeah. No problem,
no problem! I understand, it takes a while after you come
back. How was Fiji? It's nice this time of year, isn't it? Yeah.

Yeah. Fine. Keeping busy, you know. I thought maybe we could get together sometime next week, I could pitch you this thing. The Vietnam thing, you know, the one I mentioned. Oh, I thought I told you. It's a Vietnam thing, guy gets back from Vietnam and uh, his wife, his wife has gotten a job at, uh—

(Sam is snapping his fingers at Brian for notes. Brian rustles around, finds some papers, and hands them to Sam.)

SAM Uh . . . uh . . . she . . . works . . . she works at a . . . bank. She works at a bank and one day her husband shows up at work. Oh, I forgot to mention that he was in Special Forces . . . huh? Sure, take your time. I'll hold.

(Sam becomes inert, waiting for Macklin. Everyone in the room is stock still. It's as if they were waiting for something important to happen. Thirty seconds.)

SAM Yeah? Frank? Yeah. It's Sam. Sam Barry, I was telling you about . . . oh. Sure, I understand, no problem. Could we set a time now? No, sure, then I'll call you next week. No problem, I'll call next week. But I tell you it's a great—Okay. I understand. Thanks, Frank. Thanks a lot.

(Pause. Silence. Defeat.)

TOMMY   I want to be a star.

(Brian has handed Sam a copy of the script for the Vietnam flick.)

SAM   I don't need it now, you moron!

(Sam throws the script at the wall.)

SAM   What's that, Tommy?

TOMMY   I want to be a star.

SAM   Lemme tell you something, Tommy, you're gonna be a star.
You know why? Because you have talent and most of the
people in this town wouldn't know talent if it ran them over
on the highway. You've got talent because you've got heart
and you're honest. *(Pause)* I gotta take a dump.

*(Sam makes his way to his private office bathroom. Goes in, locks the
door.)*

NARRATOR   He likes you, Tommy.

SHARON   He helps people he likes.

BRIAN   Just don't get him mad.

ANDREA   Tommy, come here, let me fix your shirt! *(Pulling him close and whispering)* What's wrong with you? Don't you want to be in movies? Don't you want Mr. Barry to make you a big star? Stop acting so stupid!

(Knock on door at the same time opening. RICKY ROLLINS enters. He is handsome, cocky, and cloaked in affluence. He is nothing less than a star.)

RICKY   Hey Brian, howya doin'? Where's Sam?

BRIAN   Oh, hi, Ricky. He's, uh, stepped out.

RICKY   Taking a dump? Cool. Am I interrupting? What's going on here?

(Tommy is amazed to see Ricky in the flesh.)

TOMMY   Ricky Rollins!

RICKY   Hey there, bucky!

(The Narrator stands and extends his hand.)

NARRATOR   Trumper Morris from the WCA. We met last year on the *Last Feast* set.

Ricky   (Instantly bored) Oh yeah. Sure. How you doin'?

Narrator   Not as well as you!

Ricky   Good. That's good. We just wrapped *Muscle* this week, so
I'm kinda wasted. Two hours before my plane leaves for Fiji,
so I thought I'd come visit my pal Sam.

Narrator   How'd it go?

Ricky   Art Duckfold sucks as a director.

Narrator   He's a client of ours.

Ricky   Is he? You should get rid of him. But Tracey Toboggan.
Whew!! Hot. Nasty. Tasty. Had some every night, you know
what I mean?

Narrator   More or less.

Ricky   Probably less.

(Ricky laughs at his joke. The Narrator smiles at the putdown.
Ricky notices Andrea and Sharon at the same time.)

Ricky   Who's this? Oh, hiya Sharon.

Sharon   Hi Rick. I waited three hours at the Ivy.

Ricky   You did? Ivy at the Shore?

SHARON   No! You didn't say the shore! I was in Beverly Hills!

RICKY   Babe, I waited an hour for you, figured you hated me, and split.

SHARON   Maybe another time. The offer's still good.

RICKY   Okay. Sure.

(Sam enters, zipping his zipper.)

SAM   What offer? Nobody offers anything until I get my cut. Ricky, you look good. How's Karen?

RICKY   I don't know. She left me two weeks ago.

SAM   I'm sorry to hear that.

RICKY   Fuck her. Anyways, you're not sorry. I know you. Go take a crack at her. Knock yourself out.

(Ricky again addresses Andrea.)

RICKY   So who are you? Madonna?

(Andrea laughs at this idiotic joke.)

SAM   Rick, this is Andrea Simson, Tommy Simson's mother.

RICKY   Who the fuck is Tommy Simson?

TOMMY   I am.

RICKY   Oh. Sorry there fella. *(To Andrea)* I'm pleased to meet you, Andrea, I'm Ricky—

ANDREA   I know who you are. I'm probably your biggest fan.

RICKY   Really?

ANDREA   Uh-huh.

RICKY   Wow! Cool! That's very cool of you. What do you do?

ANDREA   I'm Tommy's mother.

SAM   Little Tommy here wants to be a big star like you, Rick. You're his hero.

RICKY   Oh yeah?

TOMMY   Not really.

ANDREA   Tommy!

TOMMY   He isn't! Johnny Depp . . .

RICKY   Cool. Cool. The whole family hates me. Sharon's the only one who loves me.

BRIAN   We all love you, Ricky.

SAM   Brian, get Rick a cup of coffee.

RICKY   I don't want a cup of coffee.

SAM   What?

RICKY   Nothing.

SAM   So?

RICKY   You know "so"!

SAM   Perrier?

RICKY   Cut the shit, Sam, tell me I'm in.

SAM   In what?

RICKY   *Memories of Monday*, what do you mean, what?

SAM   You're in it, I already made you an offer, you're in. You're in. How "in" can you be?

RICKY   Not as Cameron.

SAM   Yes, *Cameron*, that's the part for you. You'll look great.

RICKY   Sam, don't do this. You know I don't want that. *Sam.* You know what I want.

SAM Hey, Ricky, there's an old saying: Take the money and run. What are you bitchin' about? Lead role, cool cash, and two gross points. Never happy. You want me to slit my wrists?

(Ricky sits on the couch, sullen.)

RICKY You know what I want, Sam!

SAM Can you believe this, everybody? I just told this guy he's starring in a major motion picture with his name above the credits and more take home than a Lotto winner and he's crying. He's crying. It's tough being God, isn't it, Ricky? You can't get enough.

RICKY You know what I want, Sam.

SAM Yeah, I know what you want. You want the juicy little maniac role that I have all cast with somebody else who's gonna hit a home run with it *and* . . . get this everybody . . . *and* you want to direct the goddamn picture! This is in consideration of the fact that you've never directed anything in your life and you want to take *my* pride and joy, my project, fiddle with it, ruin it, and flush it down the toilet! We got a director, so forget it.

RICKY Who?

SAM Never mind who, you don't want to be in the picture, so you don't need to know.

RICKY   I didn't say I didn't want to be in it! Who's directing?

SAM   Vincent.

RICKY   Vincent! I can't believe this. I can't fucking believe this.

BRIAN   Here's your coffee, Ricky.

(Ricky takes the cup and smashes it against a wall.)

RICKY   Fuck you, Sam, fuck you! Vincent Brasnakov! Shit! And
you think I'm going to let him direct me? You think I'm a
jerk, don't you? You think you can just pull my strings and
I'll jump around for you, don't you?

(Ricky paces restlessly.)

SAM   What are you talking about? Sit down, Ricky, drink some
coffee, relax. You're a star. Brian, more coffee.

RICKY   No, I'm not a star, I'm a jerk. I'm your jerk. Until the next
one comes along. I believe you, that's my problem. I believe
you care. You take me out to lunch, you tell me I'm directing
this film, all the time you're laughing at me, inside. You're
thinking: "Sucker!"

SAM   That is not true.

RICKY   I should kick your ass!

(Ricky smashes an ashtray.)

SAM   Ricky, you're becoming irrational here.

RICKY   Oh, yeah, sure. Crazy. I'm crazy. I'm a crazy prima donna. Lunatic, unpredictable, undependable. I know what you all think about me. "Guy should be in AA. What's he on today? Better keep an eye on him!"

BRIAN   Nobody thinks that, Ricky.

NARRATOR   I can safely say you have an excellent reputation.

RICKY   What the fuck do you know? Who the fuck are you to tell me about my reputation? What do you know about reputations? You're just a pimp.

SAM   Ricky, this is getting out of hand here.

RICKY   I'm frustrated, Sam! My fiancée walks out on me so I'm at Morton's every night looking for a blow job in the coat room! And if I dare walk down the street, every tourist in town wants an autograph. I can't take a piss without giving out an autograph! And what it is, I'm fucked. My days are numbered and I know it. I just got here and I'm on the way out. The *Star* puts me on the front page and the world waits for me to jump off some tall building. The groupies sit on branches like vultures. And I don't know who the fuck I am! I'm a picture, that's all. I've turned two-dimensional!

SAM   I know. I know.

RICKY   Sam, you gotta let me direct this thing. It's my only chance at salvation, it's my only chance to become real again. Please, I'm begging, in front of all these people I'm begging!

SAM   No.

(Ricky drops to his knees.)

RICKY   On my knees!

SAM   Don't be disgusting!

RICKY   I'm begging for my life, Sam!

SAM   What's wrong with you? You on drugs?

NARRATOR   Hey, big fella. Come on, nothing's that bad, let me help you . . .

(The Narrator reaches out to Ricky and touches his shoulder. Ricky leaps up and punches the Narrator in the mouth, knocking him over the couch. Sharon runs to the Narrator. Andrea grabs Tommy.)

SAM   Ricky! You're getting homicidal here! *(He turns and scans the room.)* Everybody out of the office.

(The phone rings and Brian reaches for it.)

SAM   Leave it! Better yet, get it outside! EVERYBODY OUT!

(Everybody but Sam and Ricky have left the room.)

SAM   You just hit an agent in the mouth.

RICKY   Good.

SAM   You got problems, kid, you got your priorities mixed up.

RICKY   I'm trapped. I'm fucked. I don't want to be *me* anymore.

SAM   What in God's name are you talking about? You are famous, you are wealthy, every woman in this country wants to have your baby and suck your cock at the same time. You've got five houses, fourteen vintage automobiles, twenty-seven color TV sets. Plus, everybody is afraid of you. You're living the American dream and you're punching people in the mouth!

RICKY   Agents aren't people.

SAM   They're similar to people.

(Ricky deflates, sulks.)

RICKY   You told me I would direct this one.

SAM   YOU . . . DON'T . . . KNOW . . . HOW . . . TO . . . DIRECT.
YOU'VE NEVER DIRECTED ANYTHING BEFORE IN YOUR LIFE!

RICKY   Yeah, but you said . . .

SAM   I DON'T CARE WHAT I SAID. WHAT I SAY IS NOT THE ISSUE. THE
ONLY ISSUE IS YOU COULDN'T DIRECT A PICTURE IF YOUR LIFE
DEPENDED ON IT.

RICKY   I'll learn.

SAM   Not with my money.

RICKY   You'll be sorry.

SAM   Are you threatening me?

RICKY   I can do things.

SAM   Don't threaten me, son.

RICKY   Give me this, or—

SAM   OR WHAT? WHAT ARE YOU GOING TO DO, YOU PUFFED-UP FACE
WITH LEGS? YOU THINK YOU'RE SPECIAL? YOU THINK YOU DESERVE
SPECIAL TREATMENT? I GOT NEWS FOR YOU, SON, YOU'RE NOTHING
MORE THAN A FEW BONES IN THE RIGHT PLACE AT THE RIGHT TIME.

RICKY   I won't do the picture at all. Don't forget, I'm "the talent."
   You need me.

SAM   Talent? What's your talent?

RICKY   My acting.

SAM   You know what? Get out of here, I can't look at your
   stupid face anymore. It's depressing to think you and I are in
   the same gene pool. You don't want to be in the picture,
   don't be in it. No problemo.

*(Ricky goes over to a large vase on a table, picks it up over his head as
if to smash it on the ground. Then he starts jumping up and down with
the vase over his head like a child having a tantrum.)*

RICKY   No! No! No! No! No!

SAM   I gotta take a dump.

*(Sam goes to his private bathroom.
   Brian, Sharon, the Narrator, Andrea, and Tommy come rushing
in.)*

TOMMY   Why are you doing that?

RICKY   Brian, open the door.

(Brian opens the door.
    Ricky walks out with the vase.)

TOMMY   Mommy, did he just steal that thing?

ANDREA   He's just borrowing it.

(Flushing sounds in the next room. Sam reenters, adjusting his belt.)

SAM   Did he take the vase?

BRIAN   Yup.

SAM   Send him a bill.

(Tommy steps toward Sam.)

TOMMY   Mr. Barry, thank you very much for seeing me today. I really appreciate it. I enjoyed meeting you very much. I hope we can work together sometime, hopefully on your next project. I really admire you and I go to see everything that you do and, um—

(Tommy looks over to his mother for guidance. Pause.)

SAM   Everybody get out of the office except Mrs. Simson. I want to talk to her alone about Tommy.

(Sam walks over to his desk, pulls out a bottle and a glass, pours himself a shot. Everyone leaves but Andrea.)

SAM   Drink? No? I'll toast alone: To Tommy's future!

(Sam knocks back the drink, then stares hard at Andrea.)

SAM   Tommy is very talented.

ANDREA   Thank you, Mr. Barry.

SAM   Cut the "Mr. Barry" shit. Sam.

ANDREA   Thank you, Sam.

SAM   He has a big future in show business. If he plays his cards right.

ANDREA   I'm sorry if—

SAM   Let me finish . . . and if he gets the right breaks.

ANDREA   I'm sorry if he offended you. He's only a little boy.

SAM   And you're a big girl. Aren't you, Andrea?

ANDREA   Huh?

SAM   How badly do you want this for Tommy?

ANDREA   This is my dream.

SAM   He'll need your help.

(Long pause as their eyes lock.)

ANDREA   What do you think I should do? I'll do whatever you tell me.

(Andrea drops her eyes. Sam bursts out with a frightening gush of laughter.)

SAM   Andrea, Andrea, Andrea! You watch too much TV! What do you think I'm talking about here?

ANDREA   I . . . I don't know. Do I?

SAM   Do you? Maybe you think you know.

ANDREA   Maybe.

(Pause)

SAM I'm not that kind of guy, Andrea.

ANDREA You're not?

SAM I'm not interested in sex, at least not from you.

ANDREA Oh.

SAM I just want to have a chance to talk. To get to know one another better. Close your eyes for a minute.

(Andrea closes her eyes as Sam steps away from her, leaving her alone in the middle of the room.)

SAM I'm a very sentimental person.

ANDREA Yes.

SAM Eyes still closed?

ANDREA Yes.

(Sam sits at his desk, watching her.)

SAM I've been sentimental ever since I was very young. Even in my teens I was sentimental. I was always living in a dream world. A romantic. That's why I always loved the movies.

(Sam reaches into his desk drawers and pulls out a pair of powerful binoculars. As he talks, he focuses on Andrea, perusing her.)

SAM   I loved watching. Things on screen seemed more real than things in my life. I could feel life more deeply in a dark theater, just watching. Are your eyes still closed?

ANDREA   Yes.

SAM   They better be. For Tommy's sake.

ANDREA   They're closed.

SAM   You're a beautiful woman, Andrea. Keep your eyes closed and turn so you're facing me.

(Andrea turns. Sam keeps the binoculars to his eyes.)

SAM   I would constantly compare real life with the movies I went to see and the movies would always come out on top. So I would try to make my life like the movies. In school I played football. I won a scholarship. And when it came to girls, I dated only the ones who looked like starlets.

(Andrea is stiffening.)

SAM   I was constantly doing screen tests, so to speak. And finally I found a young lady who was a ringer for Grace Kelly. Her name was Sally Flintner. Stupid name. She didn't like me at first but I wooed her and impressed her, and then I acted like I didn't give a shit about her and, of course, she finally came to me. But even then, I wouldn't make a move. We'd take long walks back to the dorm, through the autumn leaves, and talk about philosophy. I got the hook in good.

(Sam is standing now and moving slowly toward Andrea, the binoculars still stuck to his eyes. His voice has become soft and soothing, as if he's approaching a wary animal.)

SAM   I asked her for a date and she jumped at the chance. I took her to see Hitchcock's *Rear Window*. I'd already seen it five times. We sat in the last row of the theater. That's where all the cool cats sat so they could make out. I put my arm around her; she was practically trembling with anticipation. Of course, she was a virgin. She was a beautiful, trembling virgin and she was in my arms and . . . I couldn't take my eyes off the movie. I couldn't stop watching because the real thing was up there on the screen. The celluloid Grace was up there and nobody could compare with her.

(Sam is almost nose to nose with Andrea.)

SAM   Nobody.

(Andrea opens her eyes. She sees the binoculars inches from her face and starts screaming.)

ANDREA   A H H H H H !

(Brian, Sharon, the Narrator, and Tommy rush into the office.)

TOMMY   Mommy!

ANDREA   Tommy!

(In the flurry, Sam has disappeared once again into the bathroom.)

BRIAN   Mr. Barry!

(Brian runs to the door.)

SAM *(from within)*   Everyone go away!

ANDREA   *(To the door)* I'm sorry!

(No response.
        Brian gathers the group together and all leave.
        A flushing sound and the bathroom door opens. The Narrator
emerges.)

NARRATOR   So. You've watched. Now you may leave. You may
        go eat Häagen-Dazs. You are free to go. Me? I stay. I never

leave. I can't. I'm embedded. But don't feel sorry for me. I like it, I'm a prisoner of my own free choice. I suppose I could pack it all up and move to a farm in Iowa, but somehow I feel like it would catch up with me all over again. Maybe if I never watched another TV show, or read another glossy magazine, or picked up another newspaper, I could do that. I could wake up every morning and milk the cows and pitch the hay, pat the dog and smile at the sky. I could take a deep breath and live a contented life of serene, healthy bliss. I could do all that.

But I won't.

Good night.